THE RIGHT COMBINATION

By a quarter to twelve Alex had found her way to the lunchroom of her new school. As she was balancing her tray with one hand and reaching for a carton of yogurt, someone bumped her arm. Her purse slid down onto the tray, knocking the silverware onto the floor. As Alex bent over to get it, the girl behind her bumped her other arm and she fell forward onto her knees with a loud thud.

Alex watched the vanilla yogurt drip down the front of her black suede skirt and a fresh run creep up her nylons on her right leg. *This is the absolute worst day of my entire life*, she thought.

A voice from way off in the distance seemed to be calling to her.

"What?" she mumbled, staring down at her ruined skirt in a hopeless daze.

"Excuse me," the voice went on.

Alex looked up—and there, standing in front of her, like a vision in a dream, was the most unbelievably gorgeous boy she had ever seen.

Bantam Sweet Dreams Romances
Ask your bookseller for the books you have missed

Sweet Dreams Specials

The Right Combination

Jahnna Beecham

BANTAM BOOKS
TORONTO • NEW YORK • LONDON • SYDNEY • AUCKLAND

RL7, IL age 12 and up

THE RIGHT COMBINATION
A Bantam Book/0 553 27005 2

First publication in Great Britain

PRINTING HISTORY
Bantam edition published 1988

Bantam Books are published by Transworld Publishers Ltd., 61–63
Uxbridge Road, Ealing, London W5 5SA, in Australia by Transworld
Publishers (Australia) Pty. Ltd., 15–23 Helles Avenue, Moorebank,
NSW 2170, and in New Zealand by Transworld Publishers (N.Z.) Ltd.,
Cnr. Moselle and Waipareira Avenues, Henderson, Auckland.

Printed and bound in Great Britain by
Cox & Wyman Ltd., Reading, Berks.

For May Wilson—Head Cheerleader

Chapter One

"There it is," Alexandra Clairborn whispered solemnly. "That's where we'll be spending the next two years of our lives." She stared at the mammoth brick building standing before her and shuddered involuntarily. Two years! It sounded like a prison sentence.

"Alex, I'm scared!" her best friend, Jill Tanner, whimpered, clutching Alex's arm tightly. "It's so—so *huge!*"

Alex looked up at her tall, lanky friend and grinned, her blue eyes brimming with confidence.

"Look," she began firmly, "Centennial High may be the biggest high school in Denver, but it's still only a school. So what's there to be afraid of?"

"Well, first of all," Jill said, tugging nervously at a lock of her dark, curly hair, "we won't know a soul. We'll probably wander around lost

1

all the time, we won't have any classes together, the teachers will all be mean—"

"You're right," Alex wailed. "I'm petrified!"

They burst out laughing and clung to each other, shaking with mirth. Alex noticed that their hysteria was attracting peculiar stares from other students clustered around them on the steps. She self-consciously fluffed her shoulder-length brown hair and tried to collect herself.

"Now, we've got to think positively." Alex smoothed her lace knit top over her black suede skirt and flipped up the collar of her matching short jacket. "The first day of school is hard for everyone."

"It's especially hard for us!" Jill muttered, clutching her notebook to her chest. "I don't know why the school board had to close Evergreen High and spread our class all over the city."

"Well, Evergreen was the smallest high school," Alex reasoned patiently. "When the school budget was cut, it was the logical school to close down."

"Why didn't they pick Madison High?" Jill demanded, unconvinced. "That's certainly the ugliest school."

"Look on the bright side," Alex said. "At least we got assigned to the same school, right?"

Jill nodded tentatively. Then the bell rang just above their heads, and before they knew it,

2

Alex and Jill were swept into the front hallway of Centennial High.

"All students will report to the auditorium immediately," a voice said, booming over the loudspeakers.

"Where's the auditorium?" Jill yelled over the buzzing crowd.

"I'm not sure," Alex shouted back. "But it looks like we're heading right for it." The crowd shoved and jostled toward the two sets of double doors at the end of the hall.

"Yo, Clairborn!" a voice called from behind her. Alex managed to twist around and look over her shoulder.

"Eric!" she exclaimed in surprise, waving back at a big, tousle-headed guy across the hall. "How are you?"

"Who's Eric?" Jill whispered loudly, having maneuvered her way back to Alex's side.

"He used to live on my block," Alex explained. "He moved when I was twelve. I think he's a senior here."

She neglected to mention that when he had lived in her neighborhood, Eric Nash had never given her the time of day. She was surprised that he even knew her name.

"Juniors through door B," a pleasant man in a green-and-white track suit announced. He motioned toward the auditorium with a clipboard.

"Hey, Coach Whitmore!" a broad-shouldered

boy in front of the girls spoke and waved as he went by.

Alex and Jill passed by the coach and followed everyone else into the auditorium. They found a pair of seats together on the aisle and sat down in relief.

"Look!" Jill shouted, pointing at a group of girls several rows in front of them. "Isn't that Janie Blaylock? And there's Sally Tyler, too!"

Alex peered out over the crowd in the direction Jill had indicated and recognized the two girls from Evergreen. Jill caught their attention and they waved at one another.

"Boy, it's such a relief to see familiar faces," Jill said, twisting around to see if she could spot any other friends.

A tall, balding man in a rumpled gray suit stood behind a microphone on the stage. "Is this thing on?" he mumbled, bending over and tapping the mike with his thumb. "Testing, one, two, testing. Good morning. As most of you know, I am Mr. Higgenbotham, your principal."

A loud groan came from the back of the auditorium where the seniors had staked out their territory. The principal glared in that direction, and silence quickly returned. Jill gave Alex a panicked look.

"He looks kind of mean," she whispered. "Do you think he ever smiles?"

4

Alex started to reply but something in the principal's speech made her turn her attention back to the stage.

"And because of the unexpected overcrowding this year, students will have to double up on lockers."

There was an outraged cry, and Mr. Higgenbotham barked sternly, "Now, it's only temporary, until we can get the new lockers installed. Girls will be paired with girls, and boys with boys. And I expect complete cooperation on this matter."

"Let's ask to be put together," Jill said.

"Good idea," Alex whispered back.

The principal droned on, and Alex felt her attention start to wander, until he announced, "All incoming students shall proceed directly to the cafeteria. You will receive class schedules and locker assignments there."

Alex looked up at Jill and grinned. "I guess that's us."

Alex stepped forward and faced a gray-haired woman seated behind a long table.

"Name?" the woman demanded without looking up.

"Alex Clairborn."

"What? I can't hear you." She pushed her wire-rimmed glasses up on her nose and glared at Alex impatiently.

"Alex Clairborn," she repeated carefully. The lady glanced down at a sheet of computer paper before her and ran a thin finger down a row of names.

"Clairborn—Clairborn—" she muttered under her breath. "Ah, yes, here you are. You'll have locker number five eighty-seven, and your partner will be Kris Van Dam."

Jill squeezed her arm urgently, and Alex blurted out, "Excuse me, but my friend and I would like to share a locker."

"Now, see here, young lady," the woman snapped, "we can't possibly accommodate every little request. Look at that long line behind you." Alex automatically turned and looked.

"What if everyone asked for special privileges?" the woman said, her voice growing louder. "We'd never get through the day."

Then, to Alex's horror, the woman stood up abruptly and bellowed out to the entire room, "Everyone will accept the locker assignments as given. There will be *no* exceptions." She added pointedly, "If you have any questions, you can take them up with Mr. Higgenbotham—*after* school." Then she fixed a baleful eye on Alex and said, "Is that completely understood?"

Alex nodded her head numbly. She picked up the slip of paper with her schedule and locker combination and turned away. It took every ounce of her willpower to walk calmly toward

6

the exit. Her face was burning with humiliation, and she could feel everyone staring at her.

Finally she pushed her way through the heavy doors of the cafeteria and leaned against the wall outside. Her heart was pounding and she took a deep breath, trying to calm herself.

"Oh, Alex," Jill's voice sounded beside her. "Wasn't that awful?"

"Really! That was one of the most embarrassing moments of my entire life."

"Well, if it makes you feel any better, that grouch was yelling at the person behind me when I left."

"Boy," Alex groaned. "Talk about starting off on the wrong foot!"

"Let me see your schedule," Jill said. She grabbed Alex's slip of paper and compared it to hers, muttering, "Oh, no! The only class we have together is PE, last period."

"That's too bad," Alex said, peering over her friend's shoulder. Then she added brightly, "But look, Jill, at least we're scheduled for the same lunch."

At that moment the first-period bell rang, and the hall was filled again with moving masses of students.

Alex quickly retrieved her schedule and stepped back from the crowd.

"What's your first class?" Jill asked as she

squinted up at the numbers on the nearest door.

"Mr. Schaumberg, composition and literature," Alex shouted, glancing quickly down at the little slip of paper. "Room two-oh-nine."

"I've got Mrs. Mackenzie in Room four-nineteen," Jill shouted back over the clamor. A panicked look suddenly crossed her face. "When will I see you again?"

Alex dove into the crush of students moving down the corridor to the right and yelled, "We'll meet at lunch. Good luck!"

Jill waved back feebly. Then she slipped out of sight, and Alex began looking for her classroom. All around her, students were feverishly examining and reexamining their schedules, then abruptly reversing directions. Alex smiled in spite of herself. It was a relief to know that she wasn't the only one confused by this big school.

By the time Alex realized that room 209 was on the second floor, she only had a few minutes to beat the late bell. She ran up the stairs and clattered down the hall. A stenciled sign caught her eye: Mr. Schaumberg—English Lit.

"That's the one," she muttered to herself. "Here we go!" She swallowed hard, raised her chin high, and sailed through the door just as the tardy bell rang.

There was one vacant seat at the back of the

room. Alex scurried to the desk, looped her purse over the back of her chair, and collapsed in her place before the bell had stopped ringing.

As if on cue, the man behind the desk stood up and gazed bemusedly at the class. "Greetings, one and all!" Mr. Schaumberg began. He had thinning, dark hair and an impish grin. He was wearing a red-plaid bow tie with matching red suspenders, and Alex liked him instantly. She loved literature classes, anyway, and having such a nice guy for a teacher would make English even better.

"Since 'time waits for no man,' we'll get roll call out of the way and move on to more interesting matters." He smiled out at the group and added, "I recognize quite a few old faces, but I see some refreshing new ones as well." There was a slight murmur as most of the class looked around and smiled at one another.

I must be the only new person from Evergreen, Alex thought glumly, as she looked around the class. No one looked familiar, but they all seemed to know one another.

"Shall we?" Mr. Schaumberg said, flipping open his attendance book. He reeled off the names quickly and was answered with the usual "Here!" and "Present!" and the occasional "Yo!"

Alex sat patiently and waited for her name to be called, but before she knew it, Mr. Schaumberg had gone through the *C*'s and was well into the *M*'s. Alex started to raise her hand to tell him he had skipped her name when she heard him announce "Eric Nash."

She whipped around with a start and stared at the husky football player who was sitting two aisles away.

What's he doing here? she thought. *He's a—*

As discreetly as she could, Alex groped for her purse. She felt for her schedule and tried to sneak it inconspicuously into her lap. Her hands shook a little as she stared down at the little slip of paper.

There it was, in black and white: "Mr. Schaumberg, English Lit.—Second Period!"

Then for the first time, Alex noticed the writing on the blackboard. "Senior English" was scrawled in yellow chalk across the top. She was in the wrong class. Not only was she in the wrong class, but she was in a room filled with seniors!

Alex tried to think of what to do. She just couldn't bear the thought of having to announce to the whole class that she had made such a stupid mistake. Maybe she could just get up and make a run for it. No, the door was at the front of the room, and that would mean walking past all thirty people. Maybe she could just wait out the period and then slip away without being noticed.

Alex slumped as far down in her seat as possible, staring intently at her shiny desktop. She felt each minute drag into an eternity.

"You, at the back of the class!" she heard Mr. Schaumberg call. "Yoo-hoo!"

Alex looked over her shoulder, hoping that there'd be someone behind her. Instead, she found herself looking at a poster of Mark Twain, whose amused eyes seemed to be enjoying her predicament.

"No, you! In the suede jacket."

"Me?" she asked, pointing to herself.

"Yes, you," he said, smiling at her. "I don't seem to have your name on my list."

By this time the entire class was staring at her, and Alex felt her cheeks grow hot with embarrassment. "Well—" she said, beginning in a meek little voice that seemed to come from a thousand miles away. "That's because—"

"I'm sorry," Mr. Schaumberg interrupted. "I can't quite hear you."

Alex sat up straight in her seat, squinched her eyes shut, and blurted out, "I'm in the wrong class!"

A mocking murmur ran around the class and soon turned into actual snickering.

"Well, you should have said something earlier when I skipped your name," Mr. Schaumberg remarked, looking a little confused. Alex opened her eyes and looked up at him helplessly.

He caught the pleading look in her eyes and

added gently, "I think we can straighten this out pretty easily. Tell me your name, and where you think you're supposed to be."

Alex fumbled for the schedule that she had somehow crumpled up into a tiny ball in her hands, flattened it out on her desk, and stared at it.

"My name is Alex Clairborn," she finally said. "I think I'm supposed to be in chemistry with Mr. McPhillips." She looked up at him and said, "I have you next period."

"Ah, you're a junior. From Evergreen?" Mr. Schaumberg asked with a kind smile. Alex nodded her head.

"Well, don't feel bad about the confusion, uh— Alex, right?" he said. "It takes a while to get used to a new school."

Alex tried to smile back at him gratefully, but her mouth seemed to twist crookedly all by itself.

"Well, considering that this period is short today and our time is nearly up, why don't you just stay?" he suggested, then added with a sly grin, "But tomorrow, I strongly advise you to attend Mr. McPhillips's class instead." He silenced a laugh from across the room with a dour look, then chuckled wryly. "It's certainly gratifying to know at least one person likes English lit enough to get here early."

Alex bit her lip and stared down at her desktop while Mr. Schaumberg went on with the class.

His words faded in her ears as she scolded herself for acting like a jerk.

I should have just spoken up, she thought. *Everyone in the whole class must think I'm an idiot. Including Mr. Schaumberg.*

When the bell finally rang, Alex waited until every last person had left the room before she dared to raise her head.

Her next two classes passed without a hitch, and by a quarter to twelve Alex had found her way to the lunchroom. She slipped into line behind two girls whom she recognized from her old school. They chatted for a while, and she started to get her confidence back.

Then, as she was balancing her tray with one hand and reaching for a carton of yogurt, someone bumped her arm. Her purse slid down onto the tray, knocking the silverware onto the floor. As Alex bent over to get it, the girl behind her bumped her other arm and she fell forward onto her knees with a loud thud.

Alex watched the vanilla yogurt drip down the front of her black suede skirt and a fresh run creep up her nylons on her right leg. *This is the absolute worst day of my entire life,* she thought.

A voice from way off in the distance seemed to be calling to her.

"What?" she mumbled, staring down at her ruined skirt in a hopeless daze.

"Excuse me," the voice went on.

Alex looked up—and there, standing in front of her, like a vision in a dream, was the most unbelievably gorgeous boy she had ever seen.

Chapter Two

"Are you all right?" the boy asked, his voice full of concern.

"What?" Alex asked again, mesmerized by his gray eyes. A shock of dark hair fell across his forehead as he peered into her face with eyes that had little gold flecks that sparkled in the light.

"Are you okay?" he asked again, reaching out to help her up.

"Oh!" Alex exclaimed, abruptly returning to her senses. "Yes! I'm fine." She leapt to her feet and stammered, "I guess today just isn't my day!"

"I guess not." He set the yogurt on her tray and handed it back to her with a grin.

"Thanks," Alex giggled shyly. Then she grabbed a paper napkin and furiously wiped at the stain on her skirt.

"Hey, you're holding up the line!" A voice complained from behind her.

Alex hurriedly dug into her purse for some change and paid the cashier for the remains of her yogurt. By the time she was finished, the boy had gone.

With a little sigh of disappointment, she picked up her tray again, this time making sure she had a firm grip on it, and headed for an empty table. A dreamy smile crossed her face as she replayed the last few moments in her mind.

In the midst of total disaster, a tall, dark-haired stranger had come to her rescue. The warm rumble of his voice still echoed in her memory. What color were his eyes again? Gray—or a soft hazel. It wasn't so much the color of his eyes that made them special, but the expression in them—something that blended real concern with a sense of humor.

Alex absentmindedly dug her spoon into her yogurt, lost in thought.

"Earth to Alex!" Jill said, waving her hand in front of Alex's face.

"What?" Alex asked automatically, looking up at her friend.

"I've been standing here for two minutes, watching you with that silly grin on your face!" Jill set her tray down opposite Alex and settled into her seat. "You must be having a good day."

"Good day!" Alex cried. "It's been horrendous!

I can't think of a single day in my whole life that has been worse than this one."

"Before you tell me the gory details," Jill said, "I want you to meet someone." She gestured toward a short, plump blonde who had just walked over to join them.

"Alex, this is Jennifer Trumbaugh," Jill announced. "She's my new locker partner."

"Nice to meet you!" Alex smiled at the big-eyed girl who wore red glasses perched on the end of her nose. "Which school are you from?"

"Well, actually, I'm not from around here," the girl said with a drawl. "I'm from Texas."

"Isn't that cool?" said Jill. "I used to live in Texas. And"—she paused dramatically—"we both have the same initials."

"It must be fate!" Alex proclaimed.

"That's what I was thinking," Jill said. "Anyway, we decided we'd decorate the locker door with a big *J.T.*"

Jill was talking a mile a minute while eating forkfuls of tuna salad. "We're also in three classes together."

"That's great for you guys." Alex tried to sound enthusiastic. Jill seemed to be making the transition to their new school without a hitch. Whereas Alex felt as if she had just lived through Pearl Harbor.

"Who's your partner?" Jenny asked.

"Kris Something-or-Other," Alex replied. "I

haven't met her yet." Then she slumped in her chair and said, confessing to them, "I haven't even found my locker."

"Well," Jenny said encouragingly, "I hope you're as lucky with your partner as I've been with mine."

"She will be!" Jill pronounced as she finished the remains of her tuna salad.

"Listen," Jenny said, gathering her books, "my next class is at the far end of this giant building y'all call a school. And if I don't want to be late, I'd better go!"

They watched Jenny disappear through the cafeteria doors, and then Jill turned to face Alex. "Okay, Alexandra," Jill said, folding her hands firmly in front of her. "What happened?"

Alex stared down at the yogurt stain on her suede skirt, and the morning's events rushed back to her. "Well, first of all—I got yelled at in front of the entire junior class. You were there for that. And then I got confused about my schedule and went to the wrong class. Well, it was the right class but the wrong period—and now all the seniors at Centennial High think I'm a total idiot, including Eric Nash, whom I hardly know anyway, so it shouldn't matter, but it does. And then I spilled yogurt all over my skirt, and when I tried to pick it up, I got shoved and fell on the floor in front of the entire cafeteria. And then this boy . . . ."

Alex's voice trailed off as she spotted the boy who helped her in the cafeteria line. He was talking and laughing with some guys at the very next table.

Her eyes widened, and Alex nearly shouted, "There he is!"

Jill instinctively turned to look over her shoulder, and Alex said, "Don't look!"

Jill froze in midturn, then muttered out of the side of her mouth, "Who am I *not* supposed to be looking at?"

"Only the most beautiful boy that I have ever seen in all of my sixteen years of existence on this planet!" Alex gushed, carefully picking up her spoon and dropping it into her empty yogurt cup.

"Where is this hunk?" Jill whispered, slowly turning to face Alex again.

"He's directly behind you," Alex replied, trying not to move her lips. "And if you turn around and stare at him, I'll never speak to you again as long as I live!"

Jill sat facing Alex, drumming her fingers impatiently on the cafeteria table. Finally she burst out, "I can't stand the suspense! I'm going to look!"

"Okay," Alex whispered. "But act casual."

Jill picked up her napkin and wiped her mouth with a grand gesture. Then she threw the napkin over her shoulder and made a production of twisting around in her seat to pick it up.

At the same moment the guys at the next table all stood up and headed for the double doors. Jill screeched and tried to get out of their way. When she was finally able to regain her balance, they had already gone out into the hall.

"That was subtle," Alex said wryly.

"Sorry," Jill mumbled. "I lost my balance." Her hair had gotten all messed up when she was upside down, and she self-consciously tried to pat it back into place. "Which one was he? From the angle I was at, they all looked alike."

Jill looked so flustered that Alex laughed out loud. "We'll see him again," she said, picking up her tray. "Now, come on. Help me find my locker before the bell rings."

Once they were in the hallway, Alex checked her slip of paper and followed the numbers down the long bank of green-and-white lockers leading toward the gym.

"Here it is," she cried triumphantly. "Five-eight-seven."

After fumbling a moment with the combination, Alex managed to swing the door open. Inside were two shelves and a set of coat hooks.

"Looks like she's already been here." Jill pointed to the gray warm-up jacket hanging on one of the hooks.

"Boy," Alex said, holding out one of the sleeves. "She must be pretty tall!"

"And what's wrong with tall?" Jill demanded, putting her hands on her hips.

"Nothing." Alex grinned. "But, judging from the size of this jacket, she'd make you look like a shrimp."

Jill stretched her arm out next to the sleeve. "Wow, you're right."

"She must be a jock." Alex slipped books onto the first shelf. "Anybody who brings a sweat suit to school on the first day has to be."

"Yeah." Jill laughed. "A basketball player, or volleyball. Or maybe it's her boyfriend's jacket."

"Hey, look," Alex said, her voice brightening as she noticed some books propped up on the second shelf. "She likes poetry. See, here's a book of e. e. cummings's poems."

"Great!" Jill said encouragingly. "You guys'll have lots in common."

The bell rang, and Alex swung the locker door shut with a clang. As the students started to stream into the halls again, she shouted, "Jill, I'll see you in PE, okay?"

"Ooh, my favorite class," Jill shot back sarcastically. "I can't wait."

Alex laughed. Gym had always been one of her favorite classes, but Jill wasn't very athletic and dreaded it. In fact, she was kind of a klutz,

21

all arms and legs that didn't work at all well together.

By the time Alex had reached the door of Mrs. Palmer's Algebra II class, she realized she was feeling much better about her new school.

Despite the morning's disasters she had somehow survived. Jill had made a new friend, but in time she would, too. And she had met the most handsome guy in the world—well, sort of met. Alex strode confidently into the classroom and, smiling brightly at Mrs. Palmer, took a seat in the middle of the front row.

When Alex got home to her apartment that afternoon, she was surprised to find her mother sitting cross-legged on the living room carpet intently studying two cardboard posters propped up on the couch.

"What are you doing home?" Alex asked, tossing her books onto the nearest chair. She crossed the living room and gave her mother a quick hug.

"I wanted to see how your first day at school went," Rose Clairborn replied, kissing her on the cheek. "And I'm working on a new advertising campaign that I need to think over."

Alex studied the posters for a moment. "The artwork is really clever," she said.

"You *have* to say that." Rose Clairborn stood up and smiled at Alex. "You're my daughter."

They stood for a moment, reflected in the mirror over the sofa. Alex marveled once again at how alike they looked. Both had the same light brown hair and pale skin, and her mother still had a cute, girlish figure. In fact, they could easily be mistaken for sisters.

When her parents divorced, it wasn't easy for Alex to adjust to life without her father. She remembered spending most of that first year hiding in her room, feeling angry and betrayed. But gradually she and her mother realized how much they needed each other. Gradually they had become more like best friends than mother and daughter.

"Well, how did your day go?" Rose Clairborn asked.

"Oh, Mom, it was awful," Alex moaned, thinking of her disastrous morning. Then a smile brightened her face. "And wonderful, too."

"Hold it right there," her mother announced. "I'll make us two ice-cream sodas, and you can tell me *all* about it."

Chapter Three

"It's the weirdest thing," Alex said thoughtfully as she munched on a rye cracker in the cafeteria.

"What is?" Jill asked immediately, ever curious for some new gossip.

"I still haven't met my locker partner," Alex replied. "I mean, here it is, the third day of school and we haven't so much as passed in the halls."

"You probably have," Jenny said. "Only because you've never met, you wouldn't have recognized each other."

"You're probably on completely opposite schedules," Jill added.

"I guess so," Alex said, taking another bite. "I was starting to think that she just doesn't use the locker very much, but things appear and disappear throughout the day."

"Any more huge jackets?" Jill asked with a giggle.

"No, just the same one. But she must ride her bike to school, because a bicycle helmet appeared this morning, and a sweatband, too."

"Judging from the size of her jacket, she ought to call herself 'Big Bertha' instead of"—Jill turned and looked at Alex questioningly—"what was her name?"

"Kris. Kris Van Dam."

"Alex, you should write her a note," Jill suggested.

"And say what?"

"You know, just introduce yourself and arrange a time to meet."

"Good idea," Alex said, agreeing. "I'll do that."

During fifth period, Alex hastily scribbled her note of introduction.

Dear Kris—
Hi! I'm Alex, your locker mate. We seem to keep missing each other. Right now I'm in Mrs. Palmer's Algebra II class, and is it BORING! I noticed your bicycle helmet. I was thinking of biking to school, too. Well, I just wanted to introduce myself. I'm looking forward to meeting you.
                                    Alex Clairborn

P.S. e.e. cummings is one of my favorite poets!

While Mrs. Palmer handed out the next day's assignment, Alex quickly folded the note and wrote "Kris" on the outside. She decided she'd stop by the locker just before PE and tuck it between the slats.

The sudden reminder of PE class made her groan silently. That afternoon the class would be running through a skills test, which supposedly would tell them how badly out of shape they were and how much they'd have to improve by the end of the year. Alex was not looking forward to it.

Jill had been in a panic about the test since Ms. Jencks, the PE instructor, had made the announcement the day before. In fact, Jill insisted that she was going to go home and work out with her brother Todd's weights to prepare for it.

"Jill," Alex had informed her, "it is impossible to turn terminal flab into solid granite overnight.

"Well, maybe I'll sprain something," Jill retorted defensively. "And then I'll get out of the tests."

"Maybe if you drop the weights on your head, you'll never have to take PE again."

The bell rang, snapping Alex out of her reverie. She grabbed her books, raced for her locker, hurriedly tucked the note inside, and then ran toward the gym.

Jill was already dressed in her gym suit when Alex arrived.

"What are you doing here so early?" Alex demanded, quickly pulling off her clothes.

"I figured, since I'm going to flunk this thing, anyway, I'd better try to earn points for promptness." Jill snapped up her suit and turned to face Alex.

"How do I look?" she asked, striking a pose.

"How does anybody look in these things?" Alex said, holding her own one-piece suit at arm's length and grimacing. "Like a toad."

"I bet we're the only school in Jefferson County that has to wear gym suits," Jill moaned. "It's so degrading."

"Well, at least *everyone* looks awful in them," Alex said with a laugh.

At that moment, Megan Dean, one of the cheerleaders, flounced by, her raven hair shining and bouncing off her shoulders. Alex looked at Jill and whispered enviously, "Well, *almost* everyone."

"How does she do it, anyway?" Jill asked. "She can take a shapeless, ugly, green polyester bag and make it look like a prom dress."

Alex snapped up her suit, folded her clothes,

and said firmly, "Well, let's get this thing over with."

"I'm with you," Jill agreed and promptly tripped on her shoelace. She retied it, and the two of them slouched reluctantly through the door into the gym.

Ms. Jencks had already laid out the tumbling mats. In fact, their half court of the gym looked like a small obstacle course. At the other end of the gym, the boys were going through the same procedure.

"Oh, no!" Jill moaned, clutching at Alex's arm. "I forgot we'd be joining the guys today. This is horrible!"

Alex didn't react. She was too busy thinking the same thing. Their class had spent the first part of the week separated—the boys from the girls—filling out forms and sorting through the athletic equipment that had been sent over from Evergreen High.

Ms. Jencks, a stocky woman in white bermudas and a rugby shirt, stepped out of her office and strode toward them. She blew her whistle and instructed the girls to gather around her on the tumbling mats.

"Now, today's test will measure your agility and strength."

"Oh, goodie!" Jill whispered.

"You will begin the test on the mats." Ms. Jencks looked down at her clipboard and continued. "It's really very simple—a forward dive roll, a cartwheel, a turn, and a backward roll. Megan Dean will demonstrate."

"Naturally," Alex said quietly to Jill and then rolled her eyes.

They both watched glumly as Megan performed the tumbling moves perfectly, then ended with a cute leap in the air and a slap of her thighs.

"What was *that*?" Jill whispered in a panic. "That last thing she did?"

"That's known as the 'cheerleader bounce,'" Alex answered sarcastically.

The rest of the class applauded, including the boys at the other end of the gym. Megan giggled and covered her face with her hand, acting embarrassed. Her apparent modesty didn't fool Alex for a second.

"Thank you, Megan," Ms. Jencks said, smiling at her prize pupil. "The next section is for strength."

Alex groaned. She could handle the tumbling but "strength" was her weakness.

"I want you to climb as far as you can up this rope." Ms. Jencks grabbed a thick rope hanging from a large metal hook in the ceiling.

"No way," Jill said firmly. From where they were sitting, the ceiling looked awfully far away. A ripple of concerned murmuring came from the rest of the class, and Ms. Jencks raised one hand for silence.

"Now, don't worry," she said soothingly. "It's absolutely safe. Just climb up as far as you can. There will always be someone at the bottom to spot you."

Her words didn't seem to comfort anyone, least of all Jill. "I'm just going to walk over and touch it," she grumbled. "That's all she's getting from me."

Ms. Jencks blew her whistle again and, after dividing them into four groups, instructed them to line up. Then the tests began.

At first, everyone was painfully self-conscious, but gradually, an atmosphere of mutual support came over the group. They all started cheering one another on, and Alex applauded each effort with the rest of the class.

Jill, however, had not relaxed or joined in. She became quieter by the second.

"Jill Tanner!" Ms. Jencks called out. Jill didn't move.

"Jill!" Alex whispered, nudging her with her elbow. "You're up!"

"I can't do it," Jill said, her eyes wide with fear.

"What do you mean, you can't do it? Of course you can!"

Jill shook her head vehemently. Her voice quavered as she said, "I have never done a somersault or a cartwheel in my entire life!"

"Oh, Jill," Alex said with her hand on her forehead. "I completely forgot!"

"Jill Tanner!" Ms. Jencks repeated louder, this time with a touch of irritation in her voice.

Suddenly the panic in Jill's eyes was replaced by a resigned, almost hopeless glaze. She turned to Alex and looked her directly in the face.

"Whatever happens to me," she said simply, "I will always treasure the memory of our friendship."

With that, she turned on her heel and walked swiftly toward the mat, her jaw clenched in determination.

The rest of the girls called out encouragement as she walked by. A couple of them started humming the theme music from the Olympics.

Alex watched her tall, gangly friend try to curl herself into a tiny ball. Jill sat there, gripping her knees, and then slowly rocked forward—onto her head. After some flailing of her arms and shoving off with her feet, she managed to roll over and land splayed out on her back.

"I said, a 'dive roll,'" Ms. Jencks said, objecting.

"For me—that *was* a dive!" Jill said, sending a chuckle around the class.

Then Jill leaned forward, put both hands on the mat and gave a halfhearted kick of her legs up and down. The backward roll was a little harder to fake, but she managed to very carefully sit down and then roll sideways over her shoulder. Then she galloped toward the rope, reached up, and very carefully touched it.

"I guess I have my work cut out with you," Ms. Jencks commented drily.

"You sure do," Jill said. Then, fearing her grade might suffer, she added brightly, "But I'm willing to try."

She walked back to Alex's side and smiled maliciously. "You're next."

Alex took a deep breath and approached the mat. She hurled herself into the dive roll and flew straight into the cartwheel. She paused long enough to glance over her shoulder to get her bearings, then did a neat back somersault, landing in sprightly fashion on her feet. She even threw in the "cheerleader bounce" for good measure and received enthusiastic applause.

Alex was amazed she had survived the tumbling without any major mishap. She was doing well, and she knew it. Alex threw herself full force into the rope climb.

She had been watching the others carefully and figured the best strategy would be to leap as high as she could to grab the rope. That way, if she couldn't climb any higher, she would at least have gotten some height on the leap.

Alex pushed off from the blue mat and pounded across the gym toward the rope. With each stride she gathered confidence and when she was about three feet away, she leapt into the air with her arms outstretched.

A gasp went around the group as Alex sailed

past the hanging cord and crashed directly into the padded wall behind it.

The dull *thud* of her collision still ringing in her ears, Alex slid slowly to the floor. Fortunately she wasn't hurt at all, just stunned—stunned and amazed. How on earth could she have completely missed the rope?

As soon as the girls realized Alex was all right, they burst out laughing. Loud guffaws exploded from the boys' class and bounced off the gym walls in loud, harsh echoes. To Alex, it seemed as if thousands of people were laughing at her.

"Are you okay?" Ms. Jencks asked, her brow knitted with concern. She helped a shaky Alex to her feet.

Alex was just about to answer when her face froze. There he was! The boy from the cafeteria! He was standing directly across from her, in the middle of all the other boys. He had witnessed the entire flying leap and crash landing and was laughing right along with everybody else.

"Oh, Alex, that was one of the funniest things I have ever seen!" Jill rushed over to her side with tears running down her cheeks. She stifled a laugh and said breathily, "I'm so glad that didn't happen to me! I'd have died of embarrassment!"

Alex wanted to strangle Jill. Not only had she just made a complete fool of herself in front of

33

the boy of her dreams, but her best friend was making fun of her. It was too much to bear!

Seething with anger, Alex marched right back to the blue mat and started her run all over again. This time she judged the leap perfectly and caught the rope high above her head. The adrenaline surge from her anger gave her extra strength, and she managed to climb about six feet up the rope. When she could go no farther, she glanced over to the far side of the gym.

He was standing with his arms crossed, watching her. A big, approving grin creased his face. Alex almost lost her grip when she saw his smile, but focused her concentration on sliding slowly down the rope to the floor.

The girls all swarmed around her, acting as though she had just swum the English Channel. Jill patted her on the back excitedly, exclaiming, "Way to go, Clairborn!"

Even Ms. Jencks came over and told Alex how impressed she was by her grit. Alex was floating on air.

After PE she strode back to her locker and thought again about that boy and his smile. A sudden flicker of doubt crossed her mind. Had it really been an approving smile? Or had he just been laughing at her along with the rest of the guys?

Alex decided to think positively and hope that he had been impressed. She twisted the lock in her fingers, opened the door, and grabbed her jean jacket. She was just about to slam the door when she noticed the note.

It was scrawled in pencil on a piece of torn notebook paper.

Alex,
It *is* pretty amazing that we haven't met yet, but I've been really involved with athletics. I don't have practice a week from today, Thursday. Let's meet here at 3:15 then. Okay?

See ya,
Kris

P.S. I think Mrs. Palmer is boring, too.

Alex smiled. She'd been right about the sports. Maybe Kris was on the girls' basketball team. That would explain why their schedules were so different. All her free time was probably spent on the court.

She wrote in her notebook: "Meet Kris—3:15 sharp!" Then, as an afterthought, she underlined it three times.

Chapter Four

"Where *is* she?" Alex sighed, checking her watch for the tenth time. It was the next Thursday afternoon, and the last bell had rung fifteen minutes before. She leaned back against her locker and looked down the almost deserted hall. No sign of Kris.

I'll take one more look, she thought, walking quickly to the corner. Alex looked up and down the corridor. Nothing. Being stood up was a lousy way to start off a new friendship.

Just as she was about to leave, footsteps sounded behind her. With a relieved smile, Alex turned—and froze. There, standing just ten feet away, was that boy! Her heart pounded in her chest like a jackhammer.

He glanced up and caught her eye. A trace of a smile brightened his face, and he nodded slightly in recognition.

Alex blushed and smiled back, tucking a strand of hair behind one ear. It was still damp from PE.

I must look like a wreck, she thought in horror. She made a quick dash for the bathroom at the end of the hall.

Alex stared at herself in the mirror, and her shoulders slumped forward. It was worse than she had thought. Her hair wasn't just damp, it was sopping wet and clung to her face in little wisps. To make matters worse, she had missed a button on her blouse!

"Okay," she said, reasoning with her reflection, "I can either wait here till my hair dries and ruin my best chance of talking to him. Or—" She quickly rebuttoned her blouse. "I can march right out there and hope for the best."

Alex squared her shoulders resolutely and stepped back into the hall. He was still there, leaning casually against a locker.

As the bathroom door closed behind her, he looked up in surprise and smiled warmly at her again. She mustered her courage and strolled casually toward her locker.

It's now or never, she thought. *Say something!* She took a deep breath and opened her mouth to speak—but nothing came out. Her mind was a total blank.

Panicked, she stopped dead in the middle of the hall and fumbled for a book, any book, to study. She nervously opened it and stared down at the page.

Oh, great! she thought, crossing her eyes, *Chemistry!* The words and numbers began to blur as the seconds ticked away. *This is ridiculous!* her mind screamed. *Here I am, standing in the middle of the hall pretending to study. I must look like a complete idiot.*

Alex couldn't bear the tension any longer. In one swift move, she slammed her book shut and headed for her locker. *I'll just toss my books in and make a run for it,* she decided silently.

Alex reached for the lock on number 587. Another hand got there first.

"Oops, I'm sorry," she said giggling. "I must have the wrong locker."

"Sorry, my mistake," he stammered.

They both took a step back and scanned the numbers at the top of the lockers.

Alex realized she had the right one and reached for it. His hand touched hers again. She jumped and pulled her hand back.

"There must be, uh, some confusion here," he said, looking embarrassed. "But I'm sure this is my locker."

Alex stared at the number again and mumbled out loud, "Number five-eight-seven. No, I'm sure it's mine."

He scratched his head slowly, a perplexed

look on his face. Before he could say anything, Alex decided a demonstration might get through to him. "You see," she said, swiveling the lock and throwing open the locker door, "I know the combination, and my locker mate, Kris, is meeting me here."

"What was that name again?" he asked suddenly.

"Kris, uh uh—" Alex stuttered, completely thrown. "I—think her last name is Van Dam."

"*I'm* Kris Van Dam!" he said.

"You can't be!" Alex blurted out. "You're a *boy!*"

"That's what they tell me," he said dryly.

"I mean, I'm a girl and—"

"Yeah, I see that," he said with an approving grin that made her blush noticeably.

"No, what I mean, is," Alex said, "that I am—"

"Alex Clairborn," he finished for her.

Alex nodded vigorously.

"Alex?" He repeated her name curiously.

"Well, my full name is Alexandra," she tried to explain. "But I've always been called Alex— since I was really young—" She suddenly realized she was babbling and covered her mouth sheepishly.

"Well, Alex," Kris said, cocking his head to one side, "it looks like we've got a problem."

"We sure do!" Alex said, agreeing emphatically. Suddenly her eyes widened as she remembered the smelly, damp gym suit she had tossed in the bottom of the locker. And the egg salad sandwich. It had been there for two days! Frantically, she racked her brain, trying to remember if she had left anything *else* embarrassing in there.

"I guess the best thing to do," Kris said, rubbing his chin, "is for you to go to the office tomorrow and ask them to assign you another locker."

"What?" Alex said, snapping back into the present. "What do you mean?"

"Once they hear about the mix-up," he said, "they'll straighten it out in no time."

"No, you don't understand," Alex said, her voice bristling. "I mean, why should I be the one to change lockers? Why don't you ask them to switch you?"

"Hey, calm down!" Kris said, grinning at her. "Let's try to keep this rational, okay? I mean, it's obvious that the mistake is with your name."

"I don't think it's obvious at all!" Alex glared at him.

"They must have thought you were a guy," he explained patiently. Then he shrugged his shoulders. "Besides, this is a convenient location for me."

"It is also very convenient for me," Alex retorted. She completely ignored the fact that most of the time the locker seemed miles away from any of her classes.

"Look," Kris snapped. "It's near the gym. I'm on the football team. I work out a lot."

"So?" Alex shot back. "If you're so special, why doesn't the coach give you your own personal locker?"

"That's what I'm trying to tell you," Kris countered. "Everyone on the team was assigned lockers near the gym."

Alex clenched her teeth stubbornly.

"I'm not leaving!"

"Neither am I!"

They both reached for the locker door and slammed it shut at the same time. Alex spun on her heel and pounded furiously down the hall.

Halfway through the door she realized she had left her notebook inside the locker. Alex hesitated, debating whether to leave it until the next day. Then she remembered she had to study her chemistry notes. Alex set her jaw and marched right back to the locker.

Kris was still standing there, his arms folded resolutely in front of him. Alex ignored him completely and reached for the lock. She fumbled with the tumblers and gave the door a tug. It didn't open. She paused and started over.

"Shoot!" she muttered under her breath. The combination had flown completely out of her head. And knowing that Kris was staring over her shoulder didn't help her memory one bit.

She was just about to try a third time when he stepped forward.

"Having a problem?" he asked cheerfully.

"I can't get this lock to work," she grumbled, kicking at the door in frustration.

"Allow me." Kris leaned over and deftly spun the lock to the right, once to the left, and then back again.

"*Et voilà!*" he announced, opening the locker for her.

"Thanks," she acknowledged grudgingly, reaching for her notebook. Then Alex grabbed her gym suit and swung the door shut. The suit caught in the door, and she heard Kris chuckling as she tried to free it.

"What's so funny?" Alex demanded.

He stopped laughing immediately. "Nothing. Nothing at all."

There was a loud *r-r-rip* as Alex finally managed to wrench the gym suit out of the door, nearly knocking herself onto the floor.

Kris burst out laughing again and Alex wanted to hit him. "I'm sorry," he gasped. "You just looked so funny." He put on a straight face and asked, "Do you think you can fix it?"

"Of course I can fix it!" Alex snorted indignantly. "You—you potato head!"

"Arrgh," he howled, clutching his stomach as if he'd been shot. "You got me!"

Alex turned and ran down the hall, her ears

burning with the sound of his laughter. *Potato head?* she asked herself. *Where did that come from?*

Alex paused on the school steps and let the cool air outside clear her mind. With a start, she remembered the egg salad sandwich. It was still in the locker. She wasn't about to go back for it.

It can just stay there and rot, she thought, a smug little smile on her lips. *That'll show him!*

That night Alex could hardly sit still through dinner. She was dying to call Jill and tell her everything. Even while her mother filled her in on the date she had had the night before with her new boyfriend, Julian Gamble, Alex couldn't keep her mind off her own problems.

Finally, after she'd cleared the table and helped her mother with the dishes, Alex took the phone from the hall table. She pulled it into her room, collapsed on the bed, and quickly punched out Jill's number.

When Jill heard the news, she shrieked so loudly that Alex had to hold the receiver away from her ear. "Alex, that's wonderful!"

"What's so wonderful about it?" Alex demanded. "I'm practically living with the man of my dreams—and I hate him!"

There was a long pause as Jill took a moment to digest this information. Finally she stated simply, "Well, if you feel that way about him, why don't you move?"

"That's just what he said," Alex complained. "I think he should move. He assumes that just because he's a jock, I'll give in. Well, I'm not giving an inch!"

"Those sound like fighting words," Jill said, marveling.

"You bet they are! Oh"—Alex giggled—"remember that egg salad sandwich that I didn't eat Tuesday? Well, I left it in the locker. On purpose."

"That ought to get him." Jill chortled. "Hey, maybe you should pack the locker with old food. I'm sure we've got some in our refrigerator. My mom always forgets about vegetables until they're unrecognizable."

Suddenly Alex sat up with a start.

"Wait a minute, Jill!" she said excitedly, "I think you've hit on something."

"What?" Jill asked. "A thousand and one uses for rotten leftovers?"

"Ugh, no, that's totally gross," Alex replied. "But something better."

"Like what?"

"Ooh, it's too good!" Alex laughed wickedly.

"Tell me!" Jill implored. "I can't stand the mystery!"

"I can't now," Alex said, "I have to talk to my mom about it first."

"Alex!" Jill squealed across the line in agony.

"Meet me here at my house, tomorrow at a quarter to seven sharp," Alex ordered.

"What?"

"I've got a little surprise for Mr. Kris Van Dam."

Chapter Five

When the doorbell rang early the next morning, Alex was hard at work cutting pictures out of magazines.

"Would you get that, Mom?" Alex yelled toward the kitchen. "It's Jill." She shifted the scissors and carefully trimmed around a picture of Michael J. Fox. Then Alex placed it on top of the pile she had already clipped from *Teen Screen* and other fan magazines.

"Morning, Jill," she heard her mother's tired voice saying in the entryway.

"Uh—hi," came the mumbled reply. A second later Alex looked up to see a bleary-eyed Jill amble sleepily into the living room.

"Had any breakfast?" Mrs. Clairborn asked.

"Breakfast?" Jill squinted one eye at her in disbelief. "I haven't even woken up yet. I could barely get dressed."

Mrs. Clairborn chuckled understandingly and said, "I'll get some orange juice and toast while Alex shows you her handiwork."

Jill slumped into the armchair and stared numbly at Alex, who was surrounded by stray clippings and scraps of construction paper.

"Why did you insist I get up in the middle of the night to come over here?" Jill asked.

"To help me with my strategy," Alex replied. "I figured I'd fill the locker with so much 'fru-fru' that Kris'll have to move out. He won't be able to stand it."

"So you nixed the idea of rotting vegetables."

"Too messy. This is the feminine touch." Alex grinned mischievously. "Just what those jocks can't stand."

"Hey, not a bad idea." Jill started to wake up.

Alex held up the pictures and the little red and pink hearts to which she planned to tape them. "You see, I'll paste these all over the inside." She pointed to some white eyelet lace. "Mom thought of this. We'll string it along the shelves."

"I suppose this goes on the door." Jill held up a big sign that said "Alex's Place." It was bordered with hearts and flowers and looked just like one of those "Home Sweet Home" signs.

Alex nodded. "I did that last night."

"Well, it looks pretty perfect to me." Jill yawned, then added matter-of-factly, "There's only one thing missing."

"What's that?" Alex tilted her head.

"Stuffed animals."

"Jill, you're a genius!" Alex cried, leaping up from the floor and hugging her. "I knew I could count on you!"

Alex led Jill by the hand into her bedroom and sat her on the neatly made bed. A fuzzy brown teddy bear with a red-plaid ribbon around his neck lay between the pillows. Alex picked him up, hugged him tightly to her chest, then handed him to Jill.

"Here," she said. "Hold Ed Bear." Alex stood up and scrutinized her bookshelves. They were filled with stuffed animals of every imaginable size and species. A giant panda, a little yellow moose that she had won pitching darts at a county fair, a cross-eyed giraffe—she'd kept them all.

Jill watched as Alex grabbed the chair from her oak desk in the corner and dragged it toward the bookshelves.

"Slow down, Alex," Jill said, twisting around to keep up with her. "This is too much activity for one morning."

"I knew these would come in handy someday," Alex muttered as she passed down a tattered Raggedy Andy and a stuffed rabbit missing one eye. A purple dog and a faded green frog puppet were soon added to Jill's already overfilled arms.

Alex leapt off the chair, and in a moment of inspiration grabbed her illustrated edition of *Wind in the Willows* from beside her bed, along with her *Collected Poems of Emily Dickinson* and a few paperback romances.

They marched back into the living room, stacked the toys and books on the couch, and stepped back to survey the display.

"These are going to fill your whole locker," Jill commented, sipping her orange juice. She bit into a piece of toast with a loud crunch, then mumbled, "There'll hardly be any room left for your books or coat."

"Oh, it's only for today," Alex said, reassuring her. "Once Kris gets a look at all this, I know he'll run right to Mr. Higgenbotham's office and ask for a new locker."

"Ahem." Mrs. Clairborn interrupted from the doorway, gesturing pointedly at her watch. "It's getting late. If I'm going to drive you to school, we have to leave soon."

"We get to ride?" Jill asked, really perking up for the first time. "Well, that's one consolation for having to get up at the crack of dawn."

When they reached Centennial High, only a few students had begun to gather on the front steps. The girls squeezed out of the car, their arms filled with poster board, scissors, stuffed animals, and tape.

"Now, we have to be sneaky," Alex whispered conspiratorially, as she led the way down the hall toward her locker.

"How can we be sneaky with all this?" Jill asked. "Anybody who sees us will think we're having a rummage sale."

They piled their supplies on the floor by the locker, and Alex quickly turned the combination, opening the door with an unpleasant *screech*.

"We have to work fast," Alex said, urging Jill on and peering over her shoulder. "We don't want Kris to catch us in the act."

They taped the sign to the door, draped the shelves with lace, and hung the pictures of Alex's favorite teen idols along the sides. Then they carefully arranged the dolls and stuffed animals on the shelves and floor of the locker.

Alex found her egg salad sandwich, still in its paper bag. It smelled horrible, so she picked it up and carried it gingerly across the corridor to the trash can.

"I'd say it's a work of art," Jill said, stepping back to assess their efforts. Alex reached into her purse and pulled out a perfume bottle.

"Now for the final touch—Lilies of the Valley!" She sprayed the locker with the heavy floral scent and even gave an extra squirt to the sweatsuit jacket that Kris had left on one of the hooks.

50

"He's not going to like that," Jill warned.

"That's the idea," Alex said, slipping the bottle back into her purse. "This is war, remember?"

"I guess so." Jill shrugged. "But if you ask me, this is not exactly the way to win the man of your dreams."

Alex stared at her friend. That thought hadn't occurred to her at all. She suddenly realized that this really would blow any chance she might have with Kris. She quickly shook her head and said, "He started it. Who needs a dumb jock, anyway?"

The hall was beginning to fill up with other students who were getting too curious. Alex hastily reached out and slammed the locker shut.

"Now what do we do?" Jill demanded.

"We wait."

Alex didn't realize how difficult the waiting would be. All morning long she couldn't concentrate on a thing that her teachers said. Even Mr. Schaumberg's English Lit class, which was usually a lot of fun, dragged on endlessly.

"Oh, by the way," Mr. Schaumberg announced moments before the bell, "don't forget that we'll all be going out to Red Rocks next Thursday."

The class cheered the news, and Alex paid attention. As the teacher went along the aisles passing out permission slips, he said, "The Denver Theatre will be performing Sophocles' *Anti-*

51

gone, one of the classic Greek tragedies, for the entire junior class."

Scattered groans came from around the room at the mention of the play.

"Now, don't be so closed-minded," the teacher said, admonishing them with a grin. "Who knows, you just might enjoy this dose of culture."

Alex absentmindedly slipped the paper into her purse. The bell rang and, as the desks and chairs were pushed back and everyone began to leave, Mr. Schaumberg shouted over the bustle, "Just be sure to get those slips signed and back to me before next Wednesday."

At lunchtime Jill rushed to meet Alex in the line at the cafeteria. "Has he seen it yet?" she asked breathlessly.

"I can't tell," Alex replied. She picked up her chef's salad and led the way toward their table. "I stopped by the locker after second period and nothing had changed. I wonder where he is?"

She scanned the lunchroom, looking for the familiar tall figure, but there was no sign of him.

Jill jerked her thumb in the direction of a noisy table by the window. "Have you checked the jocks' table?"

Alex looked over and spotted Eric Nash leading the raucous laughter. He caught her eye and waved two fingers jauntily. Alex groaned and turned pointedly away.

"Isn't that the guy who said 'hi' the first day of school?" Jill asked, smothering her salad with Thousand Island dressing.

"Yeah," Alex groaned. "What a jerk! He's just another mindless jock—like Kris."

"Hi, y'all," Jenny called as she slid her tray onto their table. She sat down across from Alex and whispered, "Has he murdered you yet?"

Alex laughed and shook her head. "I haven't even seen him."

"Well," Jenny said, pushing her glasses up on her nose, "I don't know about Colorado but guys in Texas would never stand for that stuff. They'd be breathing steam like bulls in a rodeo."

Alex tried to smile, but she was starting to get a funny feeling in the pit of her stomach. She pushed her half-eaten salad away from her. How mad could he get?

Alex decided to avoid her locker for the rest of the afternoon. She'd never seen a rodeo bull much less a boy breathe steam like one, but the idea didn't sound very pleasant.

Chapter Six

"Today, girls," Ms. Jencks announced as they waited for the boys to join them in the gym, "Coach Whitmore and I have a special treat for you."

"I can guess what that'll be," Jill whispered. "Push-ups, with one arm tied behind our backs."

Alex stifled a giggle and turned her attention back to Ms. Jencks.

"Since it's Friday, we thought it would be fun to learn the Virginia reel!" She smiled at the class and waited for an enthusiastic response. There wasn't one. All the girls looked down at their ugly green gym suits and moaned.

Megan Dean jumped up and linked arms with Trish Miller, one of the other cheerleaders. The two girls skipped around in a circle, singing, "Swing your partner 'round and 'round!" Megan's black hair was tied in a high ponytail, and it bounced as she moved.

"She must wash her gym suit every night," Jill said under her breath.

"Wash it?" Alex responded. "I'll bet she has it dry-cleaned. Look at the little creases."

At that moment the boys filed in from their locker room. Alex's stomach knotted up again as she realized she'd actually have to face Kris right then. Maybe if she stayed at the back of the class, he wouldn't notice her.

Ms. Jencks went over to confer with Coach Whitmore, who was plugging in the record player. Meanwhile, the boys lined up across from the girls.

"There he is!" Jill whispered.

Kris, like the rest of the boys, was wearing green-and-white gym shorts and a white T-shirt. He looked more handsome than ever, and Alex's heart involuntarily skipped a beat. She had to remind herself that he was her archenemy.

"Do you think he's seen the locker?" Jill asked, her eyes fixed on him.

"He must have," Alex whispered out of the corner of her mouth. "It's hard to tell with him, though. He always seems so cool."

Just as Coach Whitmore was asking for volunteers to demonstrate the steps, their eyes met. Kris raised his hand toward Alex in a mock salute.

"Good man, Kris!" Coach Whitmore exclaimed.

There was a moment of confusion until Kris realized he had volunteered. Reluctantly, he allowed his buddies to push him out into the center of the circle. The puzzled look on his face tickled Alex so that she started to laugh. She was laughing so hard, Jill had to slap her on the back.

"Alex Clairborn!" Ms. Jencks's steely voice echoed through the gym. "If you think this is so amusing, maybe you'd like to come up here and show us just how clever you are."

Her laughter died in her throat. Meekly, Alex inched forward, through the girls, into the center. Once again, she had totally humiliated herself in front of her class.

"Now, to begin," Ms. Jencks ordered, "I want you to face each other and hold hands."

Alex forced herself to turn toward Kris, dreading the meeting of their eyes. She felt sure he'd be furious with her.

Half wincing, she peeked into his gray eyes and was totally mystified. He grinned at her like the cat who ate the canary.

Kris held out his hands, and Alex reluctantly took hold of them. They stared at each other, intensely aware of the whole class watching them.

"The first step," Ms. Jencks said, "is a *sashay*. Like the French word for *chase*. You slide your foot to the right, and then the other catches up with it." She gestured for them to demonstrate the step to the class.

Self-consciously Kris and Alex slid along the floor. Then Coach Whitmore started the record, and the class began clapping in time to the music. As they sashayed around in a circle, Kris whispered, "Nice job!"

Assuming he was referring to the locker, Alex whispered sweetly, "I thought you'd like it!"

"Yeah." Kris grinned. "I think the safety pins are very unusual. Sort of like a punk gym suit."

"What?"

In horror Alex looked down at the torn armpit of her gym suit. There were huge gaping holes showing. She hadn't taken the time to sew it and had hastily pinned it together just before class.

"Now, link arms and skip!" Ms. Jencks shouted over the music.

Alex gingerly grabbed his arm and tried to keep her elbow close to her side. She skipped, staring straight ahead. Out of the corner of her mouth, she said, "I thought you were talking about my locker."

"*Your* locker?" he asked, letting go of her arm and suddenly switching directions on her.

"Yes." She scrambled to catch up with him. "I thought I did a nice job in making it just right for me."

They skipped around in a wide circle, and as soon as they were past the teachers, Kris whispered, "I guess you haven't been there lately."

This time Alex stopped completely. "What did you do?" she demanded, dropping her arms to her sides.

"That's for me to know and you to find out!" he said, smiling. Then he skipped off, leaving her standing in the middle of the circle without a partner.

"Alex!" Ms. Jencks called from the sidelines. "Is there a problem?"

"Ah," Alex began, "No, I—"

"Skipping is very easy," Ms. Jencks said.

Before Alex could assure her that she did indeed know how to skip, Ms. Jencks continued, "Megan will demonstrate."

Megan strode past Alex and sidled up to Kris, linking her arm through his. As they began the step she smiled up at him warmly.

"See?" Megan said to Alex as they passed by. "There's nothing to it!"

"I'd like to wrinkle her gym suit!" Alex muttered under breath.

After class Alex changed out of her gym clothes as quickly as possible. She couldn't get Megan's smug look out of her mind. Jill tried to find out what had happened on the gym floor, but Alex was too angry to explain. Not only had Megan

Dean and Kris conspired to make her look foolish, but to top it off, Kris had done something
to her locker.

Alex shoved her gym suit down into her purse
and stormed out of the gymnasium. She headed
straight for locker 587, with Jill close behind.

Her hands shook as she tried to remember
the combination. Finally, after the third try,
she flung open the door.

"Oh, *no!*" they gasped in unison.

"Cleats fell on your head?" Jenny asked, wide-
eyed. She'd answered Alex and Jill's distress
call and had joined them at Alex's house Friday
night.

"Not only cleats," Alex said, fuming, "but football pads, a pair of old tennis shoes, and every
kind of T-shirt imaginable!"

"You forgot the baseball bat," Jill interjected.
"It rolled out and hit me in the ankle."

Jill rolled up her cuff and showed them the
bruise. Then she limped dramatically around
Alex's kitchen, moaning, "The only cure for it is
fudge brownies."

"You're going to have to wait about twenty-
five minutes," said Alex.

"You should have picked up that bat and let
him have it," Jenny declared, hopping up on
one of the kitchen stools.

"He wasn't there." Alex finished putting the

eggs into the brownie mix in a big yellow bowl. "Jill and I didn't discover it until after school today."

"I guess he decided to fight fire with fire," Jenny said.

"Yeah." Alex sighed. "My whole plan has completely backfired. I thought I could force him out, but it looks like he's in there for good."

"I guess the cleat is on the other foot." Jill made the crack as she was dipping her finger into the chocolate batter. "I mean, it looks like he's going to force *you* to leave."

"No way!" Alex stated, swirling the batter around the bowl. "If he thinks I'm going to give in that easily, he's got another thing coming."

Alex poured the mixture into a greased cake pan and slid it into the oven. She pushed the door shut and continued, "What gets me is that I was so crazy about this guy."

"That's easy to understand," Jenny said in her drawl. "He *is* a real gorgeous hunk. You can't deny that."

"Jenny's right," Jill said. "He has the most beautiful hazel eyes."

"They're gray," Alex corrected her. "With little gold flecks."

Jenny and Jill exchanged amused looks, and Alex felt her face start to redden. She quickly added, "But looks aren't everything."

60

"Well, if you're going to fight with someone" —Jenny giggled—"it's much more pleasant to yell at a good-looking face."

"I don't want to fight!" Alex wailed, leading them into the living room. She flopped down on the couch, and Jill and Jenny took the two armchairs. They sat silently for a few minutes.

"I'm so confused!" Alex hid her face in her hands. "One minute I'm crazy about him, and the next minute I just want to strangle him."

"If I may make an observation," Jenny said from her corner, "I think you're going about this all wrong."

"What do you mean?" Alex lifted her head and looked at Jenny.

"Well," Jenny said, "you want him to leave the locker, right?"

"Right."

"But you want to stay on friendly terms."

"Right."

"Then the solution is obvious." Jenny shrugged matter-of-factly. Alex and Jill looked at her blankly, and she explained, "You kill him with kindness."

"Get serious!" Jill dismissed the thought with a wave of her hand.

"I *am* serious." Jenny leaned forward in her chair. "The girls in Texas have it down to a science. They bat their little ol' eyelashes and play helpless and dumb, and before you know it, those big, tough guys are eating right out of their hands."

"I hate those kinds of girls!" Alex wrinkled her nose in disgust.

"Me, too!" Jenny said, agreeing. "But extreme times call for extreme measures."

"Hey, Jenny's got a point," Jill said.

"Oh, come on," Alex protested. "I could never act that way."

"Yes, you could!" Jenny insisted. "Here, give it a try." She grabbed Alex by the arms and pulled her up off the couch. "Jill," she said, "you be Kris."

Jenny sent Jill to the center of the living room. "Now, you stand there and say hello."

Jill walked slowly over to Alex and mumbled in a deep voice, "Hi, Alex."

"Hi, Kris," Alex said listlessly.

"No, no, no!" Jenny scolded. "Here, watch me!" She stood in the middle of the room, her hands clasped demurely in front of her. "Okay, now say hello again."

"Hi ya', Alex," Jill said, this time throwing herself into the role. She strutted up to Jenny in her best imitation of a hulking football player.

"Why, Kris!" Jenny cooed, her face lighting up with a dazzling smile. "I didn't see you there. My, don't you look handsome today!"

Alex groaned from the couch and covered her face.

"Aw, shucks, Alex," Jill replied, digging her toe into the rug. "This is how I always look."

Alex snickered, and Jenny gestured emphatically for her to stop it.

"Well, I'm so glad I ran into you." Jenny looked adoringly into Jill's face. "I have the teeniest problem that I just *know* you can solve."

"What is it, Alexandra?"

"Well, I know how important this locker is to you, being a football player and all." Jenny paused to make sure Alex was watching, and then continued, "But you see, Mrs. Palmer's class is *so* far away, and, well, I just *have* to stop at my locker before PE." She fluttered her eyelashes coyly and said, "You understand that, don't you?"

"Uh-huh." Jill nodded, gamely trying to keep a straight face.

"Well, if I ask to be moved, I'll never make it to class on time. And that would just be too awful!" Then she linked her arm in Jill's and asked innocently, "What should I do?"

Alex laughed out loud, causing Jenny to throw a cushion at her. Then Jenny explained, in her normal accent, "You see, you throw the ball into his court and he, being a gentleman, will do the proper thing—move!"

"Right!" Alex said, sarcastically rolling her eyes and burying her head under the pillow.

"I think Jenny may be right," Jill said slowly.

"I mean, look at the way the guys fall all over Megan Dean. And she wrote the book on this stuff!"

Alex peered out at them from under the pillow. "I don't know," she said, her resistance wavering.

"Alexandra Clairborn, you can't be so wishy-washy," Jill said firmly. "You've got to try it at least!"

"On Monday morning you put on your frilliest outfit," Jenny said, instructing her, "and give it a try. Besides, we'll be there to back you up."

"Good idea!" Jill encouraged her.

Alex squinted her eyes, trying to think. Plan A had definitely failed. However, playing a giggly, flirtatious female was not her idea of fun. On the other hand, she had not yet concocted Plan B.

"Do I have to do the accent?" Alex asked hesitantly.

"No, that is optional," said Jenny. "Just be your sweet, adorable self, and he won't know what hit him."

"Well, maybe I'll try it," she said finally. Jill and Jenny jumped up and down, cheering.

"I said maybe!" Alex cautioned.

"Boy," Jill said, clapping her hands, "I can't wait to see Megan's face when she finds out that you can beat her at her own game."

"It really would burn her up!" Alex grinned. She was beginning to enjoy the idea.

"Speaking of burning," Jenny said, sniffing the air, "do y'all smell anything?"

"The brownies!" they exclaimed and dashed toward the kitchen.

Chapter Seven

"How'd I let myself get talked into this?" Alex grumbled, tugging self-consciously at her silky white blouse. "I feel like a geek."

She had gotten up early Monday morning and followed Jenny's instructions to the letter: multicolored peasant skirt that billowed around her knees, nylons, dainty little flats, and just a touch of blush and mascara. The coral ribbon in her hair completed the ensemble and made her feel utterly ridiculous.

In fact, the longer she stood on the steps of Centennial High, the more ridiculous she felt. She had spent the weekend psyching herself up to "charm" Kris, but her confidence was fading quickly.

Where are they? Alex wondered, peering nervously down the street. Jill and Jenny were supposed to meet her in front of the school, but there was no sign of them.

After another ten minutes had passed she decided she'd have to face Kris alone. Alex took a deep breath and marched up the steps into Centennial High.

"The sooner I get this over with, the better," she whispered determinedly to herself.

"Clairborn, wait up!" a voice boomed from behind her.

She turned around to see Eric Nash lumbering toward her.

"Oh, no!" she mumbled under her breath. He was the last person she wanted to see.

"You look really different," he said, eyeing her up and down. "What is it? A new hairdo?"

"No," said Alex. She knew that her look was different, but she didn't think it was *that* different. She decided to take the silly ribbon out of her hair as soon as possible.

"I'll carry those for you," he announced. Before Alex could say a word, he had taken her books from her and tucked them under one of his large forearms.

"Thanks," Alex said, trying to smile politely. "But I'm perfectly capable of carrying my own books."

"Don't be so touchy," he said, holding her books over his head. "Besides, it gives me a good chance to talk to you."

Alex shrugged and kept walking toward her locker. She didn't like the sound of his chuckle. In fact, she realized there wasn't much about him that she did like. And now he was going to blow her whole plan!

"Dropped in on any senior classes lately?" he asked, chiding her and nudging her with his elbow.

Alex leapt away from him and answered curtly, "No, once was enough for me."

He chuckled again and strolled beside her down the hall. Alex's mind raced as she tried to think of a way to get rid of him.

"Coming to the big game on Friday?" he asked as they finally rounded the corner.

"I didn't know there was one," she responded flatly.

"You've got to be kidding me!" Eric snapped. "There are posters all over school."

"Sorry, I don't like football," she said as they stood in front of her locker. She gestured for him to return her books.

"How about football players?" Eric put one hand above her head and leaned toward her, practically pinning her against the locker.

"Especially not the players!" she shot back, ducking under his arm. Then she turned and glared at him fiercely.

"Oh, playing hard to get, are you?" Eric gave her a sly smile and, to her surprise, reached out and tweaked her under the chin. "That's cool."

Alex jumped backward as if she had been stung by a bee and fell directly into the arms of Kris Van Dam.

"Hey, Nash! How's it going?" Kris said casually, steadying Alex with his arm.

"Couldn't be better," Eric replied. Then he turned his attention back to Alex and asked her point blank, "So—are you going to the dance with me after the game, or what?"

Alex was flabbergasted. How could Eric be so vain—and so thick?

"I—already have a date," she stammered, trying to think fast, "with, uh—"

"With me!" Kris cut in, slipping his arm comfortably around her waist. "What's the idea of asking my girl out, anyway?"

An electric current shot through Alex's body, catching her completely off guard. She quickly looked into Kris's face. Was he serious?

"I didn't know you two were dating," Eric said, sounding confused.

"We're not only dating"—Kris grinned—"we're sharing this locker!" He looked down at Alex with a mischievous twinkle in his eye and added, "Right, Al?"

"Right, Krissie," Alex replied without hesitation. The corner of his eye winced slightly when she said "Krissie," but he kept smiling.

Then to make sure Eric had gotten the point, she leaned her head against Kris's shoulder. She shivered slightly as she realized how good it felt.

"Hey, that's cool," Eric said, retreating with his hands up. "Well, listen, I'll catch you guys later."

When he had disappeared around the corner, Alex quickly released herself from Kris's arms and murmured a muffled, "Thanks."

"Anytime." Kris was grinning from ear to ear. "I mean, after all, what are partners for?"

Alex knew if she was going to try Jenny's plan, she had better do it then. She clasped her hands demurely in front of her and looked shyly into his sparkling gray eyes.

"Well, I sure do appreciate it," Alex said, starting the big speech that she had practiced. Her eyes suddenly widened in horror. She was speaking in a southern accent!

She felt her face light up like a neon sign, and she quickly turned to face the locker.

"Nash is a good guy," Kris said, assuring her. "But sometimes he comes on a little too strong."

Alex shot him a surprised look. He hadn't noticed the accent at all. In fact, he was starting to be very nice.

"Oh," Alex said playfully, "I can handle him."

"After what I saw you do in PE," Kris said, "I don't doubt it."

Alex cocked her head, confused.

"The skills test," Kris said, explaining.

"Oh, that!" Alex covered her face in embarrassment. "I don't know how I missed that rope. I guess I was concentrating so hard on jumping up high that I completely missed the target."

"I think it took real guts to try it again."

"I was just trying to save face," Alex said.

"Well, I was impressed!" He leaned his shoulder against the lockers and smiled at her approvingly.

Alex smiled back and turned to open the lock. She couldn't believe this sudden change. They were actually having a very pleasant conversation, and she didn't have to playact at all.

"Hey, Alex," Kris said, tilting his head slightly, "what do you say we call a truce?"

Butterflies were spinning around in her stomach. Kris was actually acting like the guy she had dreamed he'd be. Alex couldn't believe how great everything was going. Maybe he really would take her to the dance. She nodded vigorously and opened the door.

"Aaaagh!" Alex screamed as a huge yellow-and-black paper snake exploded out of the locker. It landed on her shoulder, and she shrieked again, trying to bat it off. Behind the snake tumbled a barrage of tennis balls, sweat socks, running shoes, and a few of her stuffed animals.

"Oooh!" she said. "Kris Van Dam, you're going

71

to get it!" Alex grabbed the snake and flung it in his direction.

"Hey!" he shouted, dodging to one side. "I forgot all about that!" He ducked as she threw a tennis shoe at him. "Honest!"

"I bet!" Alex picked up the debris that had fallen on the floor and heaved it back into the locker. "I thought you were sincere!"

"I am!" he said, protesting.

Each passing second made her even angrier for having been such a fool. How could she have let herself get so excited about him?

"You jocks are all alike!" she shouted, slamming the locker shut.

"What do you mean?" he asked.

"You've got muscles where your brains should be!"

Kris stared at her for a second and then burst out laughing, which infuriated Alex even more.

"What's so funny?" she barked.

"You are," Kris said, shaking his head.

Before Alex could respond, another voice pealed lightly down the hall. "Kris, there you are!"

Megan Dean came up and hooked her arm through his. "I was wondering if I could catch a ride home with you after practice," she said.

"Sure," Kris said with a shrug. "That's okay with me." Kris looked at Megan and then back at Alex.

"Oh, hi, Alex." Megan said. "Funny, I didn't see you there."

"I guess that's because the halls are so crowded," Alex said, glancing around the empty corridors.

"I guess," Megan said, shrugging. She didn't catch the note of sarcasm in Alex's retort, but Kris did and he shot Alex a crooked grin.

Alex bent over and retrieved her purse, which was tangled up in the snake on the floor. Megan rambled on about the game on Friday and how excited the cheerleaders were about it, but Kris kept his eyes fixed on Alex.

"Are you listening to me?" Megan asked, tugging at his arm.

"What?" Kris mumbled distractedly, finally looking down at Megan. "Oh. Yeah, sure."

"Then walk me to class and tell me what you think of my idea for the pep rally." Megan took his hand and started pulling him down the hall. As they left, she called back over her shoulder, "Interesting outfit, Alex."

Alex looked down at herself. The blouse had come untucked, her slip was showing, and the coral ribbon had fallen down across her eyebrows. And she realized that she was still holding the yellow-and-black snake in her hand.

Something very strange was happening to her. Her emotions were on a roller coaster ride. One second she was angry, the next moment mush,

73

and now a new feeling was creeping in. What was it?

Alex collapsed back against the locker as the realization hit her.

She was jealous!

"Alex!" Jill called from the other end of the corridor. "I'm so sorry! My brother was going to drive us to school but his car broke down half-way here."

Jill ran down the hallway with Jenny trotting a few feet behind her. When they reached Alex, Jill bent over trying to catch her breath.

"We ran all the way here!" she gasped.

"Did it work?" Jenny asked.

"Yeah, it worked just fine," Alex answered ruefully. "Megan Dean got the boy—and I got the snake!"

Chapter Eight

It was a perfect day for a field trip—crisp and clear. The sun shone high overhead and Alex felt her spirits lift. Three whole days had passed since she had talked to Kris, and it was starting to affect her. She was becoming nervous and irritable. On Wednesday, in the cafeteria, she had snapped at Jill for no reason at all.

Alex breathed in the autumn air and hopped aboard the yellow school bus. Jill and Jenny followed her and chattered away as they made their way down the aisle.

"I just love field trips," Jill sang. "Anything to get out of school!"

"I, myself, have never been particularly fond of them," Jenny said. "Of course, in Texas, we didn't go to see plays."

"Where did you go?" Jill asked, trying to free her purse that had caught on one of the seats.

"Oh, meat-packing plants, leather factories—you know, all those places that have something to do with cows."

"Sounds gruesome," Jill said, wrinkling her nose.

"You're going to love Red Rocks!" Alex motioned for them to head toward the backseats. "It's spectacular!"

"It's great," Jill said, snagging her purse on another seat. "All these red rocks jut out of the ground and the performance is right in the middle of them."

"It's a natural amphitheater," Alex explained as she slid in next to the window. She casually glanced out at the parking lot, and her stomach did a flip-flop. There, waiting to board the next bus, was Kris.

He was wearing a yellow oxford-cloth shirt and a faded jean jacket. The wind ruffled his hair as he raised his head to look at the sun. Alex squeezed her eyes shut and forced herself not to look at him.

She was becoming absolutely haunted by Kris. On Monday, he had joked about taking her to the dance; and for the past three days, that had been all she had thought about. Alex searched for him in the halls, in the cafeteria—even in PE. Her face flushed with embarrassment as she remembered taking her gym suit home and ironing it. It was getting ridiculous!

The four school buses followed one another up the winding road toward Red Rocks. On the curves, Alex could see the other buses strung out behind them, and once again she found herself searching the windows for a glimpse of Kris.

"Wow! Look at that, y'all." Jenny's familiar drawl was laced with excitement. Alex snapped out of her daydreaming haze and looked around her. Towering rocks of red granite loomed dramatically above them.

The buses pulled into a gravel parking lot and lined up side by side at the base of a huge cliff. Their driver swung open the door of the bus, and Mr. Higgenbotham poked his head through the opening.

After he ran over the rules for the day and reminded everyone to be back on the bus by three o'clock, the students clamored off the bus into the sunshine. The teachers herded the class up the hill and into the amphitheater.

"Well, I don't know much about theater," a familiar voice pealed out in front of them. "But as far as *Antigone* is concerned, it's all Greek to me." Megan began to laugh.

Just in front of Megan, a tall, lean figure loped along easily, hands tucked in the back pockets of his jeans. Before he even turned around to laugh along with Megan, Alex knew it was Kris. Jill had spotted him, too.

"Well, look who Megan is cozying up to," Jill said archly.

"Who?" Jenny asked, standing on tiptoe to see over the crowd.

"Kris Van Dam," Alex muttered dejectedly. "And he seems to be enjoying the attention."

A loud gong from the stage reverberated around the canyon, and six costumed figures, elaborately masked, filed solemnly onto the stage. The teachers motioned everybody to find a seat immediately. Alex vowed to put any thought of Kris right out of her mind and concentrate on the play.

"Antigone was really beautiful, wasn't she," Jill commented as they gathered up their purses after the performance. "Kind of like a Greek statue."

"Yeah," Jenny agreed, nodding her head. "But I didn't understand why she wanted to bury her brother."

"I did," Jill said. "There are plenty of times I've wanted to bury Todd—alive!"

"I thought the play was wonderful!" Alex said with a sigh. The other two stared at her as if she had lost her mind.

"I'll take a rerun of 'Dallas' over this any old day," Jenny declared.

"But, don't you see," Alex said earnestly, "that's what the play was all about—how a struggle for power can tear families apart. And how sometimes a person has to sacrifice everything, even die, to be true to her conscience."

"Could you translate that into regular English?" Jenny grinned.

"Oh, Alex!" Jill punched her on the shoulder. "You take things too seriously." She stood up and stretched. "We have some time before we have to be back at the bus. Let's go climb around on the rocks."

"I think I'll just sit here for a while." Alex was disappointed by her friends' reaction to the play and wanted some time alone to savor the whole experience.

"See you back at the bus, then," Jenny called from the steps at the end of the row.

"Remember," Jill growled, lowering her voice and twitching her right eye in imitation of the principal. "Three o'clock sharp."

The entire amphitheater was deserted in minutes. Alex could hear the other students' laughter bouncing off the cliff walls as they charged off toward the rock formations.

She got up and strolled down the stone steps toward the stage. When she reached the bottom, Alex hopped up onto the platform and stared out at the rows of empty seats.

Seeing that she was alone, Alex cleared her throat and opened her mouth to speak. But she couldn't think of a line from a play. Then she remembered an Emily Dickinson poem that she had memorized long ago.

" 'I'm nobody. Who are you?' "

Her voice echoed back to her clearly. Encouraged, she continued more boldly. " 'Are you nobody, too?' "

" 'Then there's a pair of us,' " a male voice responded from the auditorium. "Don't tell!"

Alex leapt backward, startled. She squinted up at the seats. The afternoon sun was in her eyes, and she couldn't see who had spoken.

"Your turn," the voice urged.

Alex put her hand up to shield her eyes and asked, "Who is that?"

She watched a tall figure, silhouetted darkly against the sun, make his way down the steps toward her. He stopped a couple of rows away.

"I believe the next line is, 'They'd banish us, you know,' " he said, prompting her with a grin.

"Kris!" Alex cried in astonishment. She was completely mortified that he had caught her performing.

"I-I thought I was alone," she stammered. "I mean, I, uh—" Alex nervously glanced over her right shoulder, looking for another way out of the theater. When she realized that she'd have to walk past Kris, she shrugged and said lamely, "I didn't know you liked poetry."

"What'd you think I did with my poetry books?"

he asked, keeping his distance. "Carry them around for show?"

Alex had completely forgotten about seeing the books in their locker. Of course, that had been when she thought her partner was a girl.

"No, it's just that—"

"Football players can't read," Kris said, finishing for her.

Alex started to protest, then said with a grin, "I guess you caught me."

"That's okay." He chuckled. "I had no idea temperamental people would have a soft spot for Emily Dickinson."

"What do you mean, 'temperamental'?" Alex asked.

"What would *you* call throwing a shoe at someone?"

"Oh, that." She grinned sheepishly. "I guess I do fly off the handle sometimes."

"I guess you do."

"That's the Irish in me," she admitted, giggling. "We talk first and think later. My mother's the same way."

Kris strode down the steps and sat on the first row of benches. "What about theatrical talent? Does that run in the family?"

"Unfortunately, it doesn't."

"Oh, I don't know." Kris looked up at her. "I'd say there's a spark there somewhere."

"A glimmer," Alex said, rolling her eyes. Then

she sat down on the lip of the stage and let her legs dangle over the edge. "Actually, I'm more the audience type. My mom and I try to catch as many shows as we can."

"I do, too!" Kris ran his hand through his hair and smiled. "But during football season, it's a little hard."

Alex smiled back at him. Then she stared down at her feet and confessed, "My mom has a new boyfriend, so I guess she'll be going to the plays with him now." Then she looked up at Kris and shrugged. "I don't know."

"Are your parents separated?"

"No." Alex shook her head. "They're divorced." She always hated saying that word. *Divorce.* It sounded so harsh and final.

They sat there for a moment in silence.

"So are mine," Kris said, breaking the stillness. "Or they're going to be."

The bitter tone of his voice made Alex pause.

"Is this pretty recent?" she asked gently.

Kris looked up at her hesitantly. "I guess it's been going on for years. You know, fighting behind closed doors. That kind of stuff." He gave a halfhearted laugh and shook his head. "But it sure took me by surprise." There was a catch in his voice as he tried to make a joke out of it.

"I understand what you're going through. My

parents split up three years ago, and I still don't completely understand why."

"That's just it," Kris burst out, looking at her earnestly. "Nobody's telling me anything! One moment we're all together, and the next, they announce that they're getting a divorce. Bam! Just like that!" He slammed his fist into the palm of his other hand for emphasis, and the noise ricocheted off the canyon walls.

"I kept thinking it was my fault," Alex said quietly. "And if I hadn't been around, they'd still be together."

Kris nodded brusquely and stared down at his hands.

"But, you know," Alex said, continuing, "I don't think I had anything to do with it. If anything, I think I made their decision to separate more difficult. They didn't want to hurt me."

It was the first time she had ever voiced those thoughts, and saying them out loud made her realize now that they were true.

Alex felt a cool breeze touch her face and watched it blow a lock of Kris's hair down across his forehead. Absentmindedly, he brushed it away with his hand.

Suddenly Kris stood up and folded his arms across his chest. He took two steps away from her and then turned back.

"It's not just their splitting up that's the problem," he explained. "It's which one do I go with? I mean, my dad's going to move to California and wants me to go with him."

"You can't!" Alex blurted out, then quickly covered her mouth in embarrassment.

Kris shot her a surprised look. The tiniest glimmer of a smile crossed his face, but his brow furrowed again. "And mom wants me to stay here. How do you choose?"

"I don't know," Alex said, shaking her head. "I didn't really have to. My dad travels a lot, so they decided it was best if I stayed with my mom."

Alex glanced up at Kris. He didn't say anything. His gray eyes were fixed intently on her face, as though he'd find an answer there. Alex continued carefully, "My mom and I have moved twice since the divorce. I know how hard it is to change schools."

"That's what I've been thinking. Leaving Centennial in my junior year would be really tough."

Alex fought the urge to convince him to stay. She knew it was a decision he had to make.

"Hey, Van Dam!" a voice hollered from one of the rocks high above them. "What are you hanging around down there for?"

Kris's face instantly lost its seriousness, and he grinned up at his friend.

"Alexandra Clairborn and I are thinking about joining the theater."

He leapt up on the bench and struck a dramatic pose, with one hand on his chest and the other outstretched toward Alex.

"To move—or not to move!" he bellowed around the amphitheater. "*That* is the question!"

"Just what they need," his friend shouted. "Another ham!"

"Get out of town!" Kris yelled back.

Alex giggled and then glanced at her watch. "Hey, we had better hurry or the bus will leave without us."

"Afraid to be left alone with me?" Kris raised his hands menacingly above his head. "The Wolf of Red Rocks?"

Alex squealed, and he chased her up the steps of the amphitheater. When they reached the top, Kris turned and offered Alex his hand. He pulled her easily over the final step and slightly toward him.

"Thanks," she mumbled, feeling suddenly shy.

"No," Kris said, giving her hand a gentle squeeze. "Thank *you*—for understanding."

Alex lifted her eyes to meet his. She didn't dare breathe. Kris tilted his head gently, and her heart quickened.

The roar of the bus engines broke the moment, and students appeared from every direction.

Kris kept her hand in his as they joined the crowd scrambling down the hillside. Alex was bubbling inside and could have gone on running with him forever.

When they reached the bottom, she was out of breath but exhilarated. Kris guided her straight toward his bus.

"Come and ride with me," he said, his eyebrow raised just enough to make it a question. She smiled and started to climb aboard.

Suddenly Mr. Higgenbotham blocked her way. He'd obviously overheard Kris's invitation.

"Just a minute!" he demanded gruffly. "Is this the bus you came on?"

Alex meekly shook her head.

"Then get back to your own bus!" he ordered. "Immediately! We have to keep an accurate head count." He stormed off without waiting for her response.

Kris frowned darkly at the principal, then faced Alex, who was feeling terribly disappointed. "I'll see you later, then?" he asked hopefully.

Alex nodded and watched him hop onto his bus. She turned and raced to catch hers before it pulled out of the parking lot. The door closed behind her, and she smiled as she walked down the aisle.

"Uh-oh," Jill sang out, "Alex has that dazed look again." She reached out and pulled Alex down beside her.

"It can only mean one thing," Jenny said. "Kris Van Dam."

Alex smiled knowingly.

"I knew it!" Jill said. "So that's where you've been? With him?"

Alex nodded.

"Here we've been out climbing silly rocks while all the time she's been making her move," said Jenny.

"I want to hear *every*thing," Jill demanded. "Everything!"

But Alex shook her head. She couldn't tell; their talk was their special secret.

"It looks like her lips are sealed," Jenny said, folding her arms in front of her.

Alex listened halfheartedly to them discuss ways of forcing her to talk. She leaned her cheek against the cool window and let her thoughts drift back to Kris. She was discovering more and more wonderful things about him. What would it be like to kiss him? she wondered.

Chapter Nine

"Goodbye forever," Alex cried, ripping the poster of Bruce Springsteen off the side of her locker with a flourish.

The hearts and lace soon followed her idols into a big plastic garbage bag. Alex began cramming all her dolls and stuffed animals into a cardboard box propped up beside her.

She worked quickly, trying to get it all cleaned up before the bell—and before Kris arrived. Alex started to shove her teddy bear into the box, then stopped and stared pensively at the stuffed animal.

"Ed Bear stays," she said finally, propping him up on the shelf and carefully placing her copy of Emily Dickinson's poems in his lap. She turned the box on its side at the bottom of the locker and then shut the door and waited for Kris.

Alex felt a little silly just standing there, but she had to see him before school started. Her heart quickened a few times when she mistook several guys coming down the hall for him, but Kris never appeared. When the bell rang she reluctantly headed off to her first class.

During chemistry class, nagging little feelings of doubt entered Alex's mind. Maybe Thursday at the theater had just been a fluke. Maybe he had only held her hand to be friendly. Maybe she was making a lot more out of it than she should. Alex thought of her teddy bear sitting on the shelf with the book of poetry in his lap and suddenly felt really foolish.

"Miss Clairborn!"

Mr. McPhillips's voice broke her train of thought abruptly. Reflexively, Alex shouted out a startled, "What?"

"Oh, I see you've decided to join us." He was seated on the edge of his desk, his black eyes fixed on her, unblinking. Alex thought he looked an awful lot like a lizard.

"I asked you whether you might care to enlighten us as to the name of the first element listed in the Periodic Table." He smiled smugly as if he knew that she couldn't answer.

Alex was silent and overcome with a feeling of panic. Suddenly her attention was drawn to the blond-haired boy sitting across from her. Paul Fitzgerald was quietly clearing his throat and nonchalantly tapping his pencil on an open page of his notebook. Alex glanced down subtly, and then looked Mr. McPhillips straight in the eye.

"I believe," she said clearly, "the answer is hydrogen."

"Uh, that's quite right," Mr. McPhillips replied, clearly disappointed that she had known the answer. As he turned his back to write the elemental symbol on the board, Alex looked over at Paul and mouthed gratefully, "Thank you."

As soon as class was over, she hurried back to the locker. There was still no sign of Kris. She anxiously threw open the locker door to see if he had left her a note. There wasn't one.

Alex stared sadly at the bare interior and sighed. Just as she was about to close the locker door, something caught her eye. Ed Bear still had the copy of Emily Dickinson in his lap, but tucked into the red-plaid ribbon around his neck was a little white envelope. Alex's hand shook as she carefully opened the note.

Inside were two tickets for the dance that night. On a little scrap of paper, written in Kris's unmistakable scrawl, were the words, "How 'bout it?" Alex squealed with delight and skipped down the hall.

Alex set her lunch tray down triumphantly on the table in front of Jill and Jenny. The two girls gaped at the huge slice of pizza, dripping with melted cheese, and the heaping order of french fries beside it. They compared their lunches of cottage cheese and pineapple, and then looked up at Alex with imploring eyes.

"Okay, you guys." Alex laughed. "Dig in!" She pushed her fries to the center of the table, and Jill and Jenny reached for them instantly.

"Today," Alex announced grandly, "is a day for celebration!"

"What's the occasion?" Jenny said with her mouth full.

"Don't tell me you passed that algebra exam!" Jill said, smearing her fries with catsup. "I couldn't get past the first problem!"

"No, this is bigger! Much bigger!" Alex picked up a slice of her pizza and took a big bite. She chewed slowly, savoring every delicious morsel. After dabbing at her chin with her napkin, she looked at them and announced, "I have a date!"

"What?" Jill choked. "With whom?"

"Kris, of course!" Alex rolled her eyes at Jill, then said breathlessly, "It's for the dance tonight!" She dug into her purse and pulled out a slip of paper. "He left me this note. Here, read it."

Jill wiped her hands and reached for the note. Jenny leaned over her shoulder eagerly as Jill unfolded it.

"Well, what do you think?" They both looked up at Alex, completely baffled.

91

"*This* is an invitation to a dance?" Jenny drawled skeptically.

"Oh." Alex laughed. "I forgot!" She dug in her purse again and produced the two orange tickets. "These came with it!"

Her friends scrutinized the tickets carefully. Just as Jenny was handing them back, she sang out, "Well, speak of the devil!"

Alex froze with her pizza halfway up to her mouth.

"Where is he?" she demanded.

"He was at the cafeteria door," Jill replied, reaching for another fry. "But now he's coming this way."

Alex slowly lowered the slice of pizza and whispered, "Switch with me!"

Jill started to stand up and Alex ordered, "No! I mean, your lunch!"

"Oh!" Jill said, her eyes widening with understanding. "Gladly!"

With a broad smile, she shoved her cottage cheese salad toward Alex and then slid the pizza over to her side of the table.

"No fair!" Jenny protested. "Here, take mine, too." Before Alex could stop her, she'd dumped her salad in front of Alex and was battling Jill for the pizza.

"Hi!" a deep voice sounded beside her.

Alex looked straight up into Kris's handsome face and chirped, "Hi, Kris!"

He grabbed the chair next to her, swung his leg over it, and sat with his elbows resting on its back.

"How's lunch?" he asked, gesturing at the two plates of cottage cheese sitting in front of her.

Alex glanced across at her friends and said pointedly, "Really good!"

Jill looked her squarely in the eye and with one huge bite devoured half of the pizza.

Alex scooted her chair around to face Kris, deliberately keeping her back to her friends.

"Did you get my message?" he asked, lowering his voice.

"Yes." Alex nodded shyly. She wasn't quite sure what to say next. She became even more self-conscious knowing that Jill and Jenny were watching her every move.

"Well?" Kris raised an eyebrow. "Do you want to go?"

Jill snickered. Alex ignored her friend and said, as calmly as possible, "I'd love to."

"Great!" Kris exclaimed delightedly. "Listen, meet me at the gym after the game. I can drive you home after the dance."

"Oh, do you have a car?" Jill blurted out from across the table. Kris looked over at her and then back at Alex.

"Oh, Kris!" Alex said suddenly, motioning

toward the girls. "These are two of my best friends, Jill and Jenny."

They both smiled and nodded at Kris.

"Hi," Kris said, acknowledging them both before he spoke directly to Jill. "In answer to your question—no, I don't have a car but my dad does. I think he'll lend it to me."

Alex watched Jill blush bright red and thought smugly, *It serves her right for being so nosy.*

"Hey, well, listen," Kris cut back in, standing up and shoving the chair back under the table, "I've got to get back to my lunch." He paused and looked at Alex directly. "You were planning to go to the game, weren't you?"

There was a loud guffaw from Jill. Alex gave her a resounding kick under the table.

"Of course," Alex replied, trying to sound casual. "Are you playing?"

"I think the coach is planning on putting me in," Kris said, a grin creasing his face.

"Then I'll be there!"

"Great!" Kris shoved his hands in his pockets and rocked back on his heels. Alex felt as if he were waiting for her to say something else, so she tossed her head and added, "I love football."

At the same time she kicked Jill under the table to make sure she didn't laugh again.

"Ow!" Jill shrieked, leaning over to grab her injured ankle. "That hurt!"

Kris stared at Jill, a confused look on his

face. Finally he shrugged and said, "I'll catch you later."

"Yeah," Alex replied. She watched him saunter away.

"Why'd you kick me?" Jill asked.

"Well, what's the big idea of laughing at everything I said?" Alex fumed.

"You can't stand football!" Jill stated.

"How do you know?"

"You've told me so a thousand times."

"Well, maybe I've changed my mind," Alex said firmly. "Maybe I've become a big fan, and you didn't know it."

"You may have become a big football fan," Jenny commented dryly, "but you sure don't know much about our team."

"What do you mean?" Alex asked. Jenny and Jill exchanged meaningful nods, and then erupted into a gale of laughter.

"What's so funny?" Alex demanded.

Jill posed with her hand under her chin and, in imitation of Alex, coyly purred, "Are *you* going to play?" This set off a whole new wave of giggles.

"So?" Alex snapped impatiently. "What was wrong with that?"

"Well, if you knew anything about the team," Jenny replied, wiping the tears from her eyes, "you'd know that Kris is the star wide receiver. So of course he's going to play!"

"What?" Alex sat there, dumbfounded. Her

cheeks burned hot with embarrassment. No wonder he'd had that funny look on his face!

"Everyone's been talking about him," Jill said, continuing gleefully to rub it in even more.

"He made the *Centennial News*!" Jenny flipped open the school paper to the second page and pointed to a picture. It was Kris, standing jauntily in his uniform with a ball tucked under his arm. The caption beneath it read "76ers' Player of the Week."

Alex was stunned. Suddenly she felt elevated to popular-crowd status.

"Why the sudden frown?" Jill asked.

"I guess I thought Kris just played," Alex replied slowly. "I had no idea he was important to the team. I mean—"

"Afraid you're out of your league?" Jill asked, reading her thoughts exactly.

"No!" Alex responded, a little too quickly. "Well, yes," she said, her voice muted with concern. "I mean, what do I know about football, and cheerleaders, and homecoming queens and all of that stuff?"

"You know, they're just the same as us," Jenny said in her quiet Texan drawl. "Except that some of them wear helmets, some wear matching skirts and sweaters, and some of them wear rhinestone crowns."

Alex laughed out loud in spite of herself. Jenny said, "I, for one, am just crazy about the game.

I never miss a chance to watch the Cowboys. I mean, they're all such mega-hunks!"

"Are you watching the game, or the players?" Jill asked slyly.

"What's the difference?" Jenny countered with a smile. "You can't have one without the other."

Jill clapped her hands together and cut in excitedly. "You know what? I think we should all go."

"Great idea," Alex agreed. She was starting to get excited about seeing Kris play but knew she didn't want to go alone. They made plans to have Jill's brother, Todd, drive them to the game.

On her way to class, Alex stopped at the Pep Club's table and bought a button that read "Go, 76ers." She pinned it proudly on her jacket and swept off down the hall.

Chapter Ten

"Oh, good!" Jill shouted, "we haven't missed the opening kickoff!" Alex and Jenny were lumbering behind her, laden with blankets, a picnic basket, and cushions.

"We're lucky we didn't miss the entire game," Alex grumbled as she carefully maneuvered her way through the crowd. "You took long enough to get ready."

"Well, someone had to bring the snacks and blankets," Jill said over her shoulder. "I didn't hear you guys volunteering anything."

"It's only a two-hour football game," Jenny piped up, breathing hard under the weight of the picnic basket. "You've got enough supplies here to last for two weeks."

"Jenny's right!" Alex added, following Jill up the stairs. "Who ever heard of bringing a picnic basket to a football game?"

"When it starts to get cold and you get hungry, you'll thank me," Jill intoned solemnly. She stopped about halfway up the bleachers and began making her way toward the center of the bench. Alex and Jenny followed behind her.

"This is the perfect spot," Jill pronounced, dropping her blanket, basket, and thermos onto the bench. "Not so close to the band that our eardrums get broken," she explained authoritatively. "But close enough to hear the announcer and watch the cheerleaders."

"Just who I want to watch," Alex said sarcastically.

"We are also very close to the home-team bench," Jenny said with a giggle. "In case you might want to watch one of the players!"

Alex grabbed a cushion, threatening her friend.

"If that's all you girls are interested in, you should have looked for seats by the locker room," a deep voice cut in from behind them. They all turned around to see Paul Fitzgerald and Mick Day grinning from their perch directly behind the girls.

"No fair eavesdropping," Jill said, smiling at the boys.

"What's in the basket?" Mick asked, reaching over Jenny's shoulder and pulling out a sandwich.

"No way!" Jenny protested, snatching it out

of his hand. "That's for halftime!" Then she added coyly, "If you want some, you'll just have to wait!"

"But I'm dying of hunger!" he pleaded.

Paul jumped right into the act and added, "Yeah, he's getting weaker by the second." Mick fell to his knees in a mock-faint, and Paul said earnestly, "You wouldn't deny a dying man—or his best friend—one tiny, little snack, would you?"

Alex noticed with a smile that Jenny and Jill had a brightness in their eyes that hadn't been in them a few moments earlier. She was just about to tease them about it when the team emerged from the locker room and ran onto the field. As they lined up in front of the grandstand, Alex searched up and down the row of identically clad Centennial players for a glimpse of Kris.

"How do you tell them apart?" she complained to Jill.

"Looking for anyone in particular?" Paul Fitzgerald stuck his head in between Alex and Jill and raised his eyebrows inquisitively. Alex nodded her head and started to answer, "Yeah, Kri—," then stopped short. She looked down at her shoes, blushing. When she finally looked up, both Paul and Jill were smiling at her.

"Try looking for a green-and-white jersey with the number fourteen on it," Paul suggested.

Alex scanned the row of players until she found Kris and grinned with delight.

Of course, once she recognized him, she couldn't believe she had missed him before. Kris was standing, one hand on his hip, in a characteristically casual pose. He looked as if he didn't have a care in the world. Alex suddenly started to worry about him. She knew how nervous she'd be if she had to stand up in front of hundreds of people and do anything.

After the national anthem, the teams returned to their respective benches. Kris turned around and scanned the crowd, as though he were looking for someone. Alex hoped he was looking for her and waved bravely.

At that moment, Megan Dean, in her cheerleader outfit, executed a snappy back walk-over into a split right in front of the bench, and the team stood up to applaud. Kris disappeared from sight behind them, and Alex settled back into her seat, her shoulders rounded forward in disappointment.

Once the game began, Alex busied herself trying to figure out what was going on. The action seemed to consist mostly of the two teams colliding into a confused tangle of bodies. The sound of their impact was pretty frightening, and Alex began to worry that someone, particularly Kris, might get hurt.

The two teams traded yardage, but the game

was scoreless when the buzzer rang at the end of the first half. The teams trotted off to the locker rooms.

"Is this the intermission?" Alex asked, while Jill found the hot chocolate and started to pour it from the thermos into plastic cups.

"We fans usually refer to it as 'halftime,'" Jenny said, kidding her. Then she grabbed the sandwiches out of the basket and brandished them in front of Mick and Paul's noses.

"Okay, troops," she said, "come'n get it!" As the guys eagerly unwrapped their sandwiches, Jill leaned over and whispered in Alex's ear, "See, I knew these would come in handy." She winked at Jenny and added, "Be prepared! That's the Tanner motto!"

"You guys going to the dance tonight?" Paul mumbled casually between bites.

The three girls looked at one another for a moment, then Jill said, carefully, "Well, Alex is, for sure. She's got a date. Jenny and I haven't really decided yet." Jenny nodded her head in agreement.

Alex shot her a horrified look. "You promised you'd go with—" Her words were squelched by a sharp pinch on her leg. Jenny and Jill were both giving her threatening looks. She subsided into silence.

Apparently the guys hadn't noticed a thing. They were too busy devouring their sandwiches.

Finally Mick Day finished chewing and, looking at Jenny, said, "Yeah, I guess it's no big deal."

That ended the conversation for a while. Paul broke the silence by remarking offhandedly, "Of course, it might be fun. Just to drop by, you know, for a while."

Jill nodded but didn't say anything. Jenny started to be unusually interested in the latch of the picnic basket. She kept snapping it open and shut, over and over again.

Mick cleared his throat. The girls looked up expectantly. He stared at them for a second, then took a long sip of his hot chocolate. All three heads turned to Paul, who sat up and swallowed hard. There was another long pause.

Alex couldn't stand it any longer. "Why don't we all go over together?" she suggested brightly.

"Yeah!" Paul said excitedly. "You know, just kind of check it out!"

"Great idea!" the others chorused and began to talk about the dance. Alex took a sip of her hot chocolate and breathed a sigh of relief.

As the second half began, it appeared that the game might grind on to a scoreless conclusion. Neither team could maneuver any offensive plays.

Suddenly, during a Centennial possession, there was a roar from the crowd as Kris broke free of a Washington defender, neatly caught the quarterback's pass, and sprinted off downfield. Alex was on her feet with everyone else, screaming, "Go! Go!" at the top of her lungs. Just then a Washington High linebacker appeared out of nowhere and slammed into Kris's right side. There was a sickening *thud* as their bodies hit the ground just a few yards from the end zone.

"How dare he?" Alex demanded, her voice quivering with outrage. "That's not fair! They ought to throw that guy out of the game!"

"Alex," Jill reminded her calmly, "the Washington player was only doing his job. Besides, Kris had a great run." She pointed toward the field where the other Centennial players were crowded around Kris, slapping him on the back.

When play resumed, the quarterback fed the ball to a burly player, who pounded and jammed his way through the thicket of jerseys across the goal line.

"Ol' Nash may not be a genius, but he's as strong as a bull," Mick Day commented as the extra point was kicked and the offensive team left the field.

"Nash?" Alex asked. "You mean, Eric Nash?"

"Yeah, he's the fullback who just scored the touchdown," Paul explained. Alex shook her head in frustration.

"Boy, that's lousy," she muttered. "Kris does all the work, and Eric gets the glory!" This drew a big laugh from the guys.

"The only play anyone'll remember is that fifty-three-yard run of Kris's," Paul proclaimed. "No need to worry about Van Dam. He's the hero of this game."

Eric's touchdown proved to be the only score of the game, and as the crowd shouted out the countdown for the final seconds, Alex was already thinking about the dance. She couldn't wait to see Kris and congratulate him on the game.

"You guys go on in," Alex announced just inside the entrance to the gym. "I'll wait here for Kris."

"Are you sure?" Jill asked anxiously. She moved restlessly from one foot to the other, her eyes fixed hungrily on the dancers inside.

"Sure I'm sure." Alex laughed. "You guys go ahead, I'll be fine."

Jill looked relieved and smiled shyly at Paul. He made a halfhearted gesture toward the dance floor, and she nodded nervously. They shuffled awkwardly through the crowd to the center of the gym.

Alex checked her purse for the tickets Kris had given her and then stood quietly by the door, waiting to greet her hero.

A group of players made their entrance, and Alex recognized Eric Nash's bulky frame among them. He looked surprised to see her and sauntered over to accept congratulations.

"Good game!" Alex shouted over the music. She felt obliged to say something since he had scored the winning touchdown.

"Thanks, Clairborn," he replied, reaching out to tickle her under the chin. "Where's your boyfriend?"

"I'm waiting for him," Alex answered evenly, retreating smoothly out of reach. "He must still be in the locker room."

"Nah, he left before me."

At that moment Kris appeared in the door, and Alex's face lit up. She raised her hand to wave but froze in midair. Megan Dean was right beside him. She stood on tiptoe and whispered something in his ear, which made Kris burst out laughing.

In that split second every shred of confidence that Alex had, disappeared. She began planning her escape. *I'll hide in the bathroom until the dance is over,* she decided. *Then I'll call Mom and she can come and get me.*

"Hey, Clairborn," a voice rumbled in her ear. She looked up, startled to see Eric Nash grinning smugly at her. "If you get lonely tonight, just give me a holler. I'll be around."

"Don't hold your breath," Alex replied. Then she forced herself to smile and walked resolutely toward Kris and Megan. She stopped a few feet from them, unsure of what to do.

"There you are!" Kris said. His eyes sparkled as he walked away from Megan without a backward glance. "I thought you were going to meet me outside the locker room."

"Oh," Alex stammered, "I thought we were supposed to meet here." She was so confused, she couldn't remember what they had decided. Part of her was wondering whether he said that to cover up the fact that he had come in with Megan. But it was hard to resist him when he seemed so glad to see her.

"Here's your dance ticket." Alex fumbled in her purse and produced the orange ticket.

"Great. Thanks." Kris took it and handed it to the girl at the door.

They stood there awkwardly, staring at each other. Finally Kris said, "Want to dance?"

Alex nodded and they threaded their way through the other couples onto the dance floor and faced each other.

"This reminds me of PE." Kris grinned impishly, holding out his hands. "Shall we sashay around the circle?"

Alex laughed and, taking his hands, said, "Let's follow it up with a couple of skips and a do-si-do!"

"Sounds good to me!" Kris led her in a circle

around the floor. They wove in and out of the mystified dancers.

Alex couldn't stop laughing as they promenaded through the hall. She felt exhilarated. Usually she felt self-conscious dancing, but Kris was such fun to be with, she didn't mind the stares.

As the music shifted to a slow dance, Kris cocked his head to one side and asked, "Well?"

"Well, what?"

"Did you like the game? You haven't said a word about it."

"Oh!" Alex moaned, putting her hands to her face. 'I forgot all about it!" She realized that seeing Kris with Megan had distracted her.

"Well, I like that!" Kris dropped his hands to his sides, acting crushed.

"No, what I mean is, I loved it!" she said quickly. "You were wonderful!"

"That's more like it," he said, flashing her a roguish smile.

He wrapped his arms around her waist, and they began to dance again. The slow music seemed to calm her jangled nerves, and Alex let her cheek rest on his shoulder. The music vibrated between their bodies as they swayed back and forth.

After a moment Kris leaned his head gently against hers. His hair was still damp from the shower. He whispered, "You smell good."

"Thanks," Alex murmured. "So do you. Like fresh, clean soap."

Kris burst out laughing.

"What's so funny?" Alex demanded, tilting her head up.

"You are," he said, gazing into her eyes. "You always say the strangest things."

"What's so strange about what I said?"

"Uh-oh! Here comes the temper!" He quickly twirled her away in a circle and held her at arm's length. "All I meant was that you always say what you think."

Alex stared up doubtfully into his gray eyes, wondering if that was good or bad. As if in answer to her thoughts, Kris pulled her toward him and murmured softly, "I like that."

Alex closed her eyes and lay her head on his shoulder. The moment was perfect, and she wished it would never end.

The music shifted abruptly to a fast song, and Kris grabbed her hand. "Let's go get something to drink, okay?"

"Great," Alex shouted back over the music. "I'm dying of thirst."

Kris was leading her toward the refreshment stand when Megan reappeared and attached herself to his arm.

"Kris," she said, "you promised me a dance, you know."

"I-I did?" Kris stammered, a perplexed look on his face.

Megan turned to Alex. "You don't mind if I take him away from you for one little victory dance, do you?"

"Of course not!" Alex replied. Turning to Kris, she said, "I'll get us a couple of sodas," and hurried off into the crowd before he could reply.

Just as she got in line, a hand reached out and pulled her toward the dance floor. Thinking Kris had changed his mind, she turned around, a glowing smile on her face.

"Thought you might need a partner." Eric Nash leered at her. "I see that yours is already taken."

Alex hesitated for a moment, the smile disappearing from her face. She really didn't want to dance with Eric, but it might do Kris good to see her dancing with someone else.

"Well, make up your mind," Eric said, tugging at her arm. "The song's almost over—"

"Nash," Kris said, interrupting him as he stepped in between them. "Why don't you drop back ten yards and punt?"

"Just watching over your girl, Van Dam," Eric said good-naturedly.

Alex shot him a disbelieving look, but Eric had already been distracted.

"I think I'll go 'long," Eric cracked, eyeing a

cute blond sophomore. "See you in the end zone!"

Alex rolled her eyes as she watched Eric stroll confidently away.

"There he goes," Kris muttered. "God's gift to warthogs."

Alex giggled and then casually asked, "So what happened to your dance?"

"The music was too fast for me," he replied. "What happened to my soda?"

Alex realized she had lost her place in line. She turned back to Kris and shrugged. "Eric was too fast for me."

Their laughter wiped away any trace of Eric or Megan's interruption. As they started to get back in line, Kris said, "Hey, I've got an idea. Why don't we drive somewhere for that soda?" He took her hand. "I know a great little place."

"Sure," Alex replied. "I'd better tell Jill and Jenny not to wait for me." She scanned the crowd and finally spotted them standing with Paul and Mick.

"Jill!" she yelled, trying to be heard over the noise. "Jill Tanner!"

When Jill finally looked up, she had a flushed, dreamy look on her face. Alex could tell she'd finally found a guy she really liked.

"I'm going for a soda with Kris. I'll call you later!" The music was so loud that Alex had to mime the motions of drinking a soda and dialing a phone.

Jill nodded that she understood, and when Paul turned to look at Alex, Jill gestured behind his back. She put her hand on her heart and pretended that it was beating really fast.

Alex mouthed the words, "Good luck!" and then followed Kris to the door.

As they were about to leave the gym, Alex spotted Megan Dean. She was holding court by the entrance, gesturing and tossing her shiny black hair from side to side.

She saw Kris and flashed a big smile. "Kris," she called over the music, "you still owe me a dance!"

"Sorry!" Kris called back. "I've got a date."

Megan's smile froze on her face as Alex and Kris passed by hand in hand.

" 'Bye, Megan," Alex said in passing. "See you Monday!'

Chapter Eleven

"So this is what they mean by a luxury car!" Alex said as she sank back into the plush leather upholstery. Kris's dad's car was a sleek white New Yorker, quite different from the old red Saab her mother drove. Kris shut the passenger door and went quickly around to the driver's seat.

"This is a very special car." He grinned, putting the keys into the ignition. "It talks."

As if on cue, a low female voice said, "Your door is ajar."

Kris quickly pulled his door shut and the voice said, "Thank you."

"You're welcome, Harriet," Kris replied, keeping a straight face. When he started the engine, the voice spoke up again: "Please fasten your seat belts."

Alex was stunned. She had never heard of a

talking car before. She quickly reached for her seat belt.

"What does she do if you don't fasten your seat belt?"

"I don't know," Kris said, securing his own belt. "I've never tried it. But I wouldn't want to make Harriet mad!"

"Thank you!" Harriet responded, sending them both into convulsions of laughter.

Within minutes, they were gliding smoothly along the highway. Kris flipped on the stereo, and as the melody of a dreamy ballad filled the car he started to reach out and change the station.

"Please, don't," Alex said softly. "I like it."

Kris looked over and grinned. "Kind of goes with the car, doesn't it?" he said, turning the music up a little. Alex leaned her head back against the soft upholstery and closed her eyes. It was all so romantic. A wonderful car and a gorgeous guy. She wondered what sort of elegant place Kris was taking her to.

When she heard the turn signal clicking and felt the car slow down Alex sat up.

There, looming in front of them, was a huge neon sign that flashed, "Bill and Nayda's." It hung over a tiny, chrome-plated diner with a pickup parked in front. Off to one side were two huge semis. There was nothing else for miles around.

Kris pulled off the highway and parked next to the red pickup truck. He flicked off the engine and then turned to look at Alex. His gray eyes flashed mischievously. Alex decided this had to be a practical joke and decided to play along.

"Oh, isn't this lovely," she cooed. "I hope you called ahead and made reservations."

"They know me here," Kris said confidently. "It might be tough, but I think I can get us in."

"Oh, but I'm not dressed properly," Alex protested, gesturing hopelessly at her pleated jeans and white linen blouse. She expected Kris to say, "You're right," and then pull out of the parking lot.

To her amazement, he threw open his door and said, "That's okay, I think I've got some flannel shirts in the trunk."

Before Alex could say anything, Harriet spoke up: "Don't forget your keys!"

Kris reached in for the keys. "We'll only be a little while," he told the car. "You'll wait for us, won't you?"

Alex stared expectantly at the dashboard, waiting for Harriet to respond. Meanwhile Kris had come around to her side of the car and opened the door.

"Milady?" He smiled, holding out his arm. Confused, Alex looped her arm in his. They walked across the gravel to a little door with a sign that said, "Come on in! We're always open."

As they stepped through the door of the brightly lit diner a burly man in overalls sitting at a corner table glanced up from his cup of coffee. Two other men, perched on the torn leather stools at the counter, turned their heads and stared curiously at the newcomers.

Alex felt as though they had stumbled into another era. The black- and white-checked linoleum floors, the molded Formica counters and tables, with little specks of glitter in them, even the old-fashioned jukebox blinking on and off in the corner—everything looked as though time had stopped in 1955.

There was a crash from the kitchen, followed by a screech, and then a lady who must have been in her fifties appeared behind the counter. She was wearing a coral-colored waitress outfit, with a short white apron. Her peroxided hair had been teased up into a beehive, and a pair of rhinestone-studded glasses hung from a chain around her neck.

"Well, look who's here!" she cried as she noticed the two of them standing by the door. Her face lit up into a big, toothy smile, and she shouted back over her shoulder, "Bill, it's Kris Van Dam!"

"What? Speak up!" barked an irritated voice from the kitchen. "I can't hear you!"

"Just drop what you're doing, and get out here!" she bellowed. "It's Kris!"

"Well, why didn't you say so!" came the reply, which was followed by another loud crash of pots and pans. Flashing a big smile, Kris grabbed Alex's hand and led her to the counter.

As the tiny woman hugged Kris, a short, round man with a moustache and a huge paunch emerged from the kitchen. He clapped Kris on the back.

"Alexandra Clairborn," Kris announced formally, "I want you to meet two of my favorite people—Bill and Nayda Burdine."

"Any friend of Kris's is a friend of ours!" Bill said, shaking Alex's hand.

"Bill!" Nayda said, jabbing him with her elbow, "you're going to wrench that poor girl's arm off." Then she looked at Alex and added, "We always get excited when we see Kris. We're just so proud of him!"

Nayda slipped her arm around his waist and said, "We heard the game on the radio tonight."

"A fifty-three-yard run!" Bill shouted to the other customers in the diner.

The two guys at the counter looked suitably impressed, and there was applause from the man at the corner table.

Kris smiled sheepishly. "That's why we're here—to celebrate. I thought I'd treat Alex to a

Nayda Special." He turned to Alex and explained, "Nayda makes the best hot cinnamon rolls in the whole state of Colorado!"

"Oh, Kris," Nayda said modestly, swiping at him with her dish towel. "Now, you know that's not true." Then she leaned over and whispered confidentially to Alex, "He's just a big flirt, but we love him!"

Before Alex knew it, Nayda had seated them at a table and put two cups of steaming hot chocolate down in front of them.

"Bill!" she called over her shoulder. "Drop a couple of quarters in the jukebox!" Then she winked at Kris and Alex. "Liven this graveyard up a bit!"

Alex and Kris laughed as they watched her scurry off to whip up her "special."

"What do you think?" Kris whispered, his eyes shining.

Alex felt as if she had suddenly been let in on a delightful secret. "I think they're wonderful!"

"I thought you'd like them." He reached across the table and held her hand. "And I knew they'd like you."

"How'd you ever find them?"

"My parents discovered this place about ten years ago, and we've been coming here ever since." A frown crossed his face, and he admitted a little sadly, "Lately, I've been visiting on my own." Then he perked up again and added, "They're kind of like my surrogate grandparents."

Just then Nayda reappeared, balancing two plates upon which sat the biggest cinnamon rolls Alex had ever seen.

"These are enormous!" she gasped, her eyes widening.

"Now, I don't want to hear any foolishness about your being on a diet," Nayda lectured. "Your figure is just perfect. Am I right, Kris?" She looked over at Kris for support.

"She's perfect!" Kris agreed emphatically.

Nayda, Bill, and Kris watched anxiously as Alex took her first bite. The roll was dripping with fresh butter, and the frosting melted in her mouth. Alex chewed slowly, savoring every morsel, then looked up at their expectant faces.

"Heaven!" she pronounced. Nayda's face spread into a wide, satisfied grin, and she patted Kris on the shoulder, urging him to dig in.

Kris and Alex attacked their rolls with a vengeance, smiling at each other as they chewed. The diner, at first so stark and cold, now seemed an oasis of warmth and friendliness. Alex realized that she had never felt so comfortable with a boy before.

When Kris tried to pay, Bill and Nayda refused indignantly.

"This is the first time Kris has ever brought a

girlfriend here," Bill announced solemnly. "And we consider it a great honor!"

Nayda smiled her agreement.

Kris turned a little red faced. Then Nayda hugged Alex goodbye and tucked a little white bag into her hand.

"For a picnic tomorrow!" she whispered, with a wink. Alex peeked into the bag and saw two more cinnamon rolls inside.

"Now, come by more often," Bill said as he and Nayda walked them out to the car.

"That's right," Nayda said. "Don't be a stranger."

Alex and Kris got into the car, promising to return soon. They couldn't stop laughing the whole way to Alex's house. Not because anything was particularly funny, but because they were so happy.

At the door they stood silently for a minute, not wanting to say good night. Then Kris took both of Alex's hands in his and gazed into her upturned face. His expression was suddenly serious.

"I really like you, Alexandra Clairborn," he said gruffly.

"I really like you, too," she whispered softly.

Then he shook his head and grinned at her crookedly. "This is going to make my decision even harder."

Alex knew what he was talking about, and the

thought of his moving away made her eyes suddenly fill with tears. She didn't know what to say.

Kris smiled sadly, then gently kissed her on the forehead. He looked down into her eyes again. "Tonight was great," he said. "I'll call you tomorrow, okay?"

Alex nodded. He wrapped his arms around her waist and kissed her tenderly on the lips. Alex felt her knees suddenly go weak, and the world spin around her.

"Good night, blue eyes," he whispered gently, then turned and reluctantly walked down the steps.

Alex floated up the stairs to her apartment, clutching the little white bag from the diner.

Chapter Twelve

"I'll get it!" Alex called from her bedroom and dashed through the door to the living room. She stubbed her toe on her dresser and, howling with pain, hopped toward the phone. She let it ring once more while she composed herself, and then carefully picked up the receiver.

"Hello?" she said, in her most sultry voice.

"Oh, hello, Alex," a British accent greeted her. "Is your mother in?"

"Hi, Julian," Alex replied, recognizing her mother's boyfriend's voice and trying not to sound disappointed. "Just a minute, I'll get her."

She handed the phone to her mother with a meek smile and flopped onto the couch.

Alex had waited all day Saturday for Kris to call, but the phone had only rung twice—both calls from Jill. The first was to discuss in minute detail every wonderful thing that had happened to them on Friday night. Jill and Paul had really hit it off. The girls spoke enthusiastically about the possibilities of double-dating.

The second call came hours later and had a completely different tone.

"Has yours called yet?" Jill asked anxiously.

"No," Alex moaned. "I'm in agony!"

"Me, too!" Then Jill abruptly cried, "They may be trying to call us right now. We'd better hang up!"

They both slammed down the receivers without even saying goodbye.

By Sunday afternoon, Alex was numb. The newspaper was strewn all over the living room floor, and Alex idly thumbed through the funnies. She had never thought about it before, but the funnies really weren't very funny. Then she flipped to the horoscope, found her sign and read it out loud.

"Believe it or not, you're ahead of schedule. Relationships are on-again off-again, and that's okay. Friendship can be more valuable than a fleeting romance."

Alex tossed the paper on the floor and complained, "That's *not* what I wanted to hear."

"What are you grumbling about?" her mother asked, hanging up the phone.

"These horoscopes. They never tell you what you want to hear." Alex hoisted herself off the couch and wandered into the kitchen. She opened the refrigerator and stared inside, her arms resting on the door. Nothing.

"Sorry there's not much in there," her mother apologized from the living room. "I haven't had a chance to go shopping."

"I'm not really hungry," Alex muttered as she shuffled across the floor toward her bedroom. Passing the telephone table, she paused and stared down at the phone.

"A watched pot never boils," said Mrs. Clairborn.

"What does that mean?"

"It means, waiting by the phone is not going to make it ring."

Alex stuck her tongue out and then marched into her bedroom and shut the door. Just as quickly she turned and went back into the living room.

"Why doesn't he call?" she asked her mother.

"Maybe something came up," Rose Clairborn said.

"What could possibly come up? He said he would call tomorrow!" She picked up a pillow and punched it. "Well, tomorrow has now become yesterday!"

"That's the old Alex spirit," her mother said with a laugh. "I thought something had happened to you."

Alex paused with her fist clenched over the pillow and stared at her mother.

"You've been moping around the house for two days," Mrs. Clairborn explained. "I thought you were getting sick."

"I have not been moping!" Alex protested.

"What do you call it, then? Here it is almost four o'clock in the afternoon and you're still in your nightgown."

Alex glanced at her blue and white flowered nightgown and said, "Maybe I am getting sick."

"Oh, you're sick all right," her mother observed. "I'd say you're lovesick."

Alex started to object again but stopped herself and collapsed back into the armchair. Basil, the cat, sprang into her lap and snuggled under her arm.

"I recognize the symptoms," Mrs. Clairborn added, a little more gently. "If he hasn't called, there's probably a very good reason."

"Like what?" Alex asked, hoping for a comforting and logical explanation.

"Well, for instance, does Kris have our phone number?"

"Of course he has our num—" Alex sat up with a start. She had never even thought about it. "Oh, no!" she wailed. "I never gave it to him!"

"Well, that could be your problem right there."

"Yeah, but he could look it up," Alex said, not about to let Kris off the hook.

"We're unlisted," Mrs. Clairborn said, crossing her arms in front of her.

"Well—he could have called Jill or Jenny and asked them for my number. They're listed."

"Do you really expect him to dial every one of your friends?" her mother asked, raising a skeptical eyebrow.

Alex thought for a second, then blurted out defiantly, "Yes! If he really cared, he would!"

"Oh, Alex," her mother replied, shaking her head. "I think you're asking a little too much."

"Besides, if he couldn't call me," Alex said, "he could have come over. He *does* know where I live."

"I think you're being ridiculous." Mrs. Clairborn stood up and stated, "As I see it, you can do one of two things."

"What?"

"Well, you can either call him—"

"Oh, no, I couldn't do that!" Alex said hastily.

"Or you can get dressed and go out with me for pizza!" her mother suggested, her eyes alight with mischief.

"Oh, Mother!" Alex muttered impatiently and started to storm away. Then she stopped. She realized she was famished. And there really wasn't anything in the refrigerator.

"Okay, you're on!"

"Put on some clothes," her mother said. "We'll leave in five minutes!"

Alex started for her room but hesitated by the phone.

"What if he somehow gets our number and calls while we're gone?" she asked anxiously.

"Then he'll know that you have better things to do than sit around the house waiting for a phone to ring!"

"Right!" Alex smiled. "If he misses me—tough luck."

"That's the spirit!"

Alex quickly pulled off her nightgown and changed into a pair of jeans and a sweater. *Boys can only make you feel bad if you let them,* she told herself, her jaw set firmly. Alex ran a brush through her hair, snatched up her purse, and turned off the bedroom light as she went out.

After they had locked the door to the apartment, Alex paused, giving the phone one last chance to ring. Then she tossed her head defiantly.

"Let's go!" she said, linking her arm through her mother's. "It's Girls Night Out!"

When Alex got to school on Monday morning, Jill was waiting by her locker.

"Alex, I've got the best news!" Jill shouted as she came toward her. "Paul finally called!"

"When?" Alex demanded.

"Last night! At exactly four minutes after eight."

"Jill, that's terrific!" said Alex.

"Did Kris call you?" Jill asked.

"No," Alex said, rolling her eyes. "Like an idiot, I forgot to give him my phone number! We're unlisted, you know."

"You're kidding!"

"Yeah, wasn't that dumb?" Alex laughed. "Besides," she added hastily, "my mother and I went out last night, so no one was home, anyway."

Alex didn't want to dwell on the subject of Kris and turned the conversation back to Paul. "So," she asked, "what did he say?"

Jill smiled smugly and announced, "He asked me out on a genuine, official date!"

At the word *date* she squeaked and grabbed Alex by the arm. The two of them hopped up and down, oblivious of the stares that they were attracting.

"Where are you going to go?" Alex asked, catching her breath.

"Well, it's nothing really big," Jill said shyly. "We're just going out for a soda after school today."

"That's why you're wearing a dress!" Alex said in amazement. Jill never wore dresses. She'd also put on lipstick and mascara. "You really look fabulous!"

"I don't know—" Jill said, tugging nervously at the belted waist of her red knit dress. "I went through a dozen outfits before I finally settled on this one."

While they talked Alex kept an eye peeled for Kris.

"The best thing about Paul," Jill announced, "is that he's three inches taller than me." She leaned against the bank of lockers and sighed happily. "I mean I have to, like, look up to talk to him."

Alex listened with only one ear, concentrating on working her combination. When she opened the door, Kris's down vest was there, hanging on the first hook. Alex quickly looked at Ed Bear, to see if any message had been tucked beneath his ribbon.

She frowned uneasily. If he was already at school, why hadn't he waited to talk to her?

"Anything wrong?" Jill asked.

"No," Alex said, trying to sound happy. "I just noticed that Kris is already here. See?" She reached out and held up his vest. "This is his."

Before Alex could hang the vest back on its hook, Jill said, "Wait, Alex, something fell out of his pocket."

Alex stared at the pink envelope lying in Jill's hand. "Kris" was written on the outside.

"Oh, it's that scented stationery!" her friend said, waving it in front of her nose. "Smells like roses."

Alex grabbed for it, but Jill held it out of reach above her head.

"I wonder who it's from?" Jill said. "Must be female because guys sure don't use stationery like this."

"Come on, Jill, cut it out," Alex said a bit impatiently. The knot in her stomach had started to tighten.

"Should we peek?" Jill whispered.

Alex hesitated. She didn't want to admit that her own curiosity was getting the better of her. At that moment the bell rang, signaling the first class of the day. She quickly snatched the envelope and tucked it back into Kris's vest pocket.

The pop quiz in chemistry prevented her from thinking about the note for the next hour. Alex fought her way through a confusing combination of ions and molecules and turned in her paper just before the bell. Then she hurried toward her locker, hoping to see Kris before the next class.

Once again the halls were crowded. As she joined the mass of students, Alex spotted his tall, lanky frame in front of her.

"Kris," she yelled excitedly. He didn't seem to hear her so she quickened her pace, ducking between a couple who had stopped to chat in the center of the hall. She started to call to him again, but the words caught in her throat. In the swirling confusion she hadn't noticed the girl walking beside him. They appeared to be deep in conversation. Alex watched them walk past her locker without stopping.

At the end of the corridor Kris caught Megan by the elbow and they stopped for a moment. Megan was speaking very quickly, and Kris leaned in closer in order to hear her. Then they disappeared out of sight around the corner.

Alex felt all the color drain from her face and her knees lock. A horrible thought passed through her mind. *It can't be!* she thought frantically. *He wouldn't! Not with her!*

"Hey, come on. Keep moving," a voice said, complaining behind her. She responded automatically and moved to the side of the hall. All she could see in her mind was that awful image of Kris and Megan together. Alex abruptly made her decision.

"I've got to know for sure," she said grimly and turned toward their locker. Alex dreaded what she might find when she reached the locker.

In a daze she spun the lock and stiffly opened the door. Kris's down vest hung on the hook, and her fingers felt inside the pocket. The little pink envelope was still there.

Hardly breathing, Alex slipped the scented notepaper from the envelope and stared at the words written on it.

Dear Kris—

Yesterday was special!
Love, M.

Alex carefully refolded the note and tucked it neatly back in Kris's pocket. Mechanically, she shut the door of the locker and turned to walk away.

A strange sound rushed in her ears, and she felt dizzy. Another student bumped into her in the hall, but Alex hardly noticed the apology that followed. She found her way to the girls' bathroom and splashed some cold water on her face.

Maybe I've got it all wrong, she thought desperately. *It's just a note from Megan. Maybe it's all one sided.*

"Yesterday was special," she recalled silently. *That doesn't sound very one sided to me!*

Alex remembered the way Megan had hung all over Kris when he had arrived at the dance, and how she had chatted with him in PE and on the way to Red Rocks.

That also explains why he never called me, she thought. *And I sat around like an idiot all weekend actually thinking he'd call!*

Her chin started to quiver, and she slapped her hand against the sink, holding back the tears that stung her eyes.

"I will not cry!" she vowed out loud. Alex snatched up her purse and pushed her way back into the hall.

Chapter Thirteen

By lunchtime Alex couldn't bear it any longer. She had kept her feelings dammed up inside her all morning, and she was ready to explode.

She stood outside the swinging doors that led into the cafeteria, trying to summon the nerve to go inside. She had deliberately avoided her locker all morning, and she didn't want to risk the chance of running into Kris now.

"Going in?"

Alex turned to see Paul Fitzgerald smiling down at her. His blond hair fell over one eye as he held the door open for her.

"I-I'm not sure," Alex stammered, stepping back from the door. "I wanted to find Jill."

"Jill should be in there," Paul said, letting the door swing back, "We decided we might eat lunch together today."

"Oh?" Alex said, her spirits sinking.

"Yeah," Paul replied, digging his hands in his pockets shyly. "We sort of talked about it in history."

He leaned against the door and held it open once again. This time Alex spotted Jill over at their usual table, talking animatedly with Jenny. From the expression on Jill's face, Alex knew they must be discussing the boys.

Alex quickly stepped out of view. "Listen, I just remembered," she said hurriedly to Paul, "I left my notebook in Mr. Schaumberg's class. Pretty dumb, I know." She laughed nervously and backed away down the hall. "Tell Jill I'll see her later, will you? And have a nice lunch."

She hoped her voice sounded casual enough because her insides felt like Jell-O. Alex managed a jaunty wave and scurried away from the cafeteria. Before she knew it, she found herself in front of the pay phone by the school office.

Alex peered nervously over her shoulder as she fumbled for a coin and slipped it into the slot. Quickly she punched in a number. After many rings, someone finally answered.

"Good afternoon," a woman's voice sang out cheerily, "Maclean Advertising."

"Mom?" Alex had expected to hear the receptionist.

"Alex! What a surprise!" her mother said cheerfully. Alex could hear music and a confused babble of voices in the background.

"Mom, I want to—"

"Honey, you'll have to talk louder," her mother broke in, "We're having a little party here."

"A party? In the middle of the day?"

"Yes!" she repeated excitedly. "Henshaw and Birkett loved my campaign! We got the account! Print and media!"

"Mom, that's fabulous!" Alex cried.

"Hold on a minute." Her mother covered the phone and shouted, "Could you keep it down to a loud roar? My daughter's on the phone."

The noise subsided slightly, and her mother asked, "Alex, is anything wrong?"

"No, no!" Alex said, in her cheeriest voice. She wasn't about to spoil her mother's excitement. "I had a few minutes between classes and just wanted to say hi!"

"Well, I'm glad you called."

"Listen, Mom," Alex said quickly, "I'll let you get back to your party. I'll see you tonight, okay?"

"Oh, honey, I won't be home for dinner. We're going to the Brown Palace to celebrate."

"Wow, pretty fancy!"

"Yeah," her mother said enthusiastically. "I think there's some lasagna in the freezer. Pop that into the microwave, and I'll see you around ten."

Alex hung up and leaned her head against the receiver. Everybody's life was going well except hers.

With a heavy sigh, she picked her books up off the floor, slung her purse over her shoulder, and dragged herself to her next class.

"Alex!" a voice called from behind her as she neared the gym. "Alex, wait up!"

She didn't need to turn around to know who it was. She had been dreading this moment all day. Alex quickened her pace, weaving her way through the crowded hall.

"Hey, where you headed so fast?" Kris said, finally catching up to her. "A fire?"

Alex couldn't bring herself to look at him, and defiantly she kept her eyes straight ahead.

"Listen, I have to talk to you. Will you slow down?"

Alex ignored him and kept on walking. Kris caught her elbow and asked, "What's the matter?"

"Nothing's the matter," Alex said shortly, pulling away. "I am on my way to class, that's all."

Kris edged around in front of her, blocking her way.

"Something is bugging you," he said. "And you're not going anywhere until you tell me what it is!"

Alex clutched her notebook to her chest and looked angrily into his gray eyes. His brow furrowed with concern as he studied her face.

"So, are you going to tell me what's wrong?"

he asked in a quiet voice. His face seemed so open and caring that her anger started to die down.

Then Alex remembered the note and the whole weekend spent waiting to hear from him. "There is absolutely nothing wrong," she said stiffly. "You decided not to call me and that's totally fine."

"Look, I'm sorry about that." Kris sighed, running his hand through his hair. "I've been trying to find you all morning. I had a really good reason—"

"I bet you did!" Alex said, cutting him off.

The abruptness of her response surprised Kris. He stepped back. "Aren't you even going to let me explain?"

"I really don't think it's necessary."

"Well, I do!" he said, eyes flashing. "And if you're going to be so pigheaded—"

"Pigheaded?" Alex shouted, her composure completely shattered.

"Yes, pigheaded," Kris shot back. "I'm trying to tell you that I was with—"

"I know who you were with," Alex cut in sarcastically. "And I don't really care."

Kris winced as though she had slapped him in the face. He stared at her, stunned. "I can't believe you're saying this," he muttered, shaking his head. "I thought you, of all people, would understand."

"How can you expect me to understand?" Alex asked.

Kris didn't answer. He just kept staring at her. Alex searched his face, trying to read his expression. Why did he look so sad? He was the one who had hurt her!

The bell rang, breaking the silence. Without another word, Kris turned and walked away.

Alex was still in shock when she reached the gym. She didn't understand that hurt look in his eyes. Had she done something wrong?

"Where have you been?" Jill demanded as they changed into their gym suits. "I waited for you in the cafeteria, but you never showed up."

"I needed to be by myself," Alex said quietly, staring at herself in the mirror. "I had to think."

Jill stood behind her, brushing her hair.

"Jill?" Alex asked, looking at her friend in the mirror. "Do you think I'm pigheaded?"

Jill paused in mid-brush. "Where did that come from?"

"Oh, it's just something I overheard." Alex didn't want to describe her fight in front of the rest of the girls. "I mean, I know I have a temper sometimes—"

"You sure do!" Jill agreed, a little too quickly.

"Okay, okay. But I'm not really pigheaded, am I?"

"Does this have something to do with Kris Van Dam?"

"Well, sort of—" Alex hesitated for a moment, checking to see if anyone was in hearing distance. Then she just blurted it out. "He makes me so mad," she said, grabbing Jill's brush and pulling it through her hair. "He doesn't call when he says he will. He doesn't come by."

Alex slammed the brush down on the counter and turned to face Jill. "He said he's been trying to get ahold of me. Well, he knows where my classes are. If he had really wanted to, he could have found me."

She was just about to break the news about Megan and the note, when Jill interrupted. "Not today, he couldn't."

"What do you mean?"

"Haven't you heard?" Jill asked. "It was all over the cafeteria."

"What?"

"Coach Whitmore and the entire football team were called into Mr. Higgenbotham's office late this morning. The coach from Washington High came over and he was steaming mad."

"Why?"

"After the dance on Friday night, some of the guys from the team went over to Washington High and spray-painted the school."

"How did he know that they were from Centennial?"

"Because some idiot wrote, 'Ha! Ha! you lose!' and 'Seventy-sixers are number one!' on the bricks of their gym."

"Sounds like something Eric Nash would do," Alex said.

"The rumor is"—Jill lowered her voice—"that he *was* the instigator, but no one is talking. I guess nobody wants to be a fink."

Alex shrugged. "So?"

"So all the players are in trouble—Higgenbotham is threatening suspension—unless they can prove where they were after the game Friday night." She paused dramatically. "That includes Kris."

At the mention of his name, Alex felt herself blush. "What does that have to do with me?" she asked coolly.

Jill stared at her in disbelief. "Well, you're his alibi."

At that moment Megan came by. She wore a ponytail up on the side and a pink-and-white sweatband around her forehead. Alex watched silently as she disappeared into the gym.

"If he needs an alibi," Alex said very matter-of-factly, "he should ask his girlfriend. I'm sure Megan can talk him out of trouble."

"What are you talking about?" Jill asked, perplexed. "You know he wasn't with Megan on Friday night."

"So?" Alex put her hands on her hips and challenged her friend.

"So you should help him out. It's only fair."

"*Fair!*" Alex shouted. "Was he being fair to lead me on and make me humiliate myself?"

141

"What's got into you?" Jill asked, stepping back to stare at her. "He doesn't call because you don't give him your number, and he can't see you because he was in the principal's office and—"

"Why are you defending him?" Alex asked, her eyes burning with tears. "I thought you were my friend."

"I am," Jill snapped back. "But sometimes, Alex, you make it very difficult!"

With that, Jill stormed off toward the exit. As she swung the door open, she shouted back over her shoulder, "And in answer to your question—yes, I do think you're pigheaded!"

The door slammed behind her with a terrible bang. Alex sat numbly in the heavy silence. She had never felt so alone in her life. Her feelings were so jumbled and confused, she didn't know what to do. No one understood what she was going through, least of all herself. Her mother was too busy for her, her best friend was mad at her. Alex didn't know where to turn.

The confusion finally overwhelmed her and a flood of hot, wet tears streamed down her cheeks. Sobbing uncontrollably, Alex collapsed into a miserable heap and held her head in her hands.

Chapter Fourteen

Alex took a deep breath and pushed open the glass doors leading into the principal's office. She had tossed and turned all night long, finally dropping off into a restless sleep just before dawn. But when she had woken up that morning, Alex had known what she had to do.

She hesitated for a second, then squared her shoulders and walked straight up to the front desk. Alex had made her decision and was going to stick to it. She was going to tell the principal the truth about Friday night.

"May I help you?" the receptionist asked mechanically. Alex felt butterflies in her stomach as she recognized the same old grouch she'd encountered on her first day of school. The name plate on the desk said "Miss Wray" and the white-haired woman looked out at her dourly from behind it.

"Yes," Alex said firmly. "I'd like to speak with Mr. Higgenbotham."

"The principal is a very busy man," the secretary snapped. "Perhaps I can help you." She picked up her pen and asked, "What's your name?"

"Alexandra Clairborn." Alex made sure to give her complete first name. She didn't want any confusion.

The receptionist carefully wrote down her name and then asked, "And what is this in reference to?"

"Well, it's about Friday night—"

"Oh?" the woman broke in, narrowing her eyes at Alex.

"I just wanted to say," Alex spoke quickly, "that Kris Van Dam was with me Friday night. So he shouldn't be punished for something he didn't do." Abruptly, Alex turned to leave.

"Just a minute, Ms. Clairborn!" Miss Wray's voice boomed, stopping Alex in her tracks. She turned around, and the receptionist gestured toward the big couch beside the door.

"Have a seat," she ordered. Then, as an afterthought, she added, "Please."

Alex did as she was told while Miss Wray pushed the button on her intercom.

"Mr. Higgenbotham?" she called. "Alexandra Clairborn is here and would like to speak with you. She says she was with Kris Van Dam on Friday night."

"Oh?" The principal's voice sounded tinny through the speaker. "Miss Wray, find Kris Van Dam and have him brought to this office."

Alex slid down in her seat. She had known it wasn't going to be easy, but she never dreamed they would summon Kris! She began to get very nervous.

The intercom crackled again. "And send Ms. Clairborn in immediately!"

"Alexandra?" the secretary said primly. "Mr. Higgenbotham will see you now."

"Thank you," Alex said weakly, trying to hold on to what was left of her courage. She stepped across the room and knocked lightly on the principal's heavy oak door.

"Come in!" an authoritative voice sounded from within. Alex swallowed hard and turned the doorknob.

Mr. Higgenbotham, wearing a rumpled blue suit and matching tie, was looking through papers at his desk. He glanced up, barely acknowledging Alex. She got the definite feeling that coming to see him was a big mistake.

"Have a seat." The principal gestured toward a straight-backed wooden chair facing the front of his desk.

"Thank you," Alex said meekly. Her legs felt

shaky, and she was relieved to know she wouldn't have to stand up very much longer.

"So," the principal said, staring at her over his glasses, "you say Kris Van Dam was with you on Friday night." The doubting tone in his voice made her feel as though she were the one being accused.

"Yes, sir," Alex mumbled. "He was."

"Now, I want you to start from the very beginning." Mr. Higgenbotham folded his hands in front of him on the desk. "Tell me everything you did on Friday night."

All of a sudden Alex felt as if she were a suspect in a detective movie about to have a bright light shone in her face to force a confession out of her. She started talking as fast as she could.

"Well, you see, sir, Kris and I went to the dance. Oh, before that, I watched the game with my friends, Jenny and Jill. Kris played in the game. Then we all went to the dance, and Paul asked Jill out. I guess that doesn't matter," she said and shook her head nervously.

Mr. Higgenbotham stared at her, and she went on with her story.

"Anyway, Kris and I danced to a couple of songs and then we went out for a soda. In his dad's car. It's a Chrysler New Yorker that talks. Well, it doesn't actually *talk*, but if you leave the door open, it will say things like 'Your door is ajar' or 'Don't forget your keys' . . ."

Her voice trailed off uncertainly as Alex realized she was just babbling. Mr. Higgenbotham was starting to look very bewildered. Alex took a deep breath and tried to get control of her nerves. Then she leaned forward and continued earnestly.

"Anyway, we stopped at a roadside diner. Well, it's more of a truck stop, actually, called Bill and Nayda's. Kris talked to the car, called her by—"

"Now, just a minute!" the principal interrupted. "Please just stick to the story." Mr. Higgenbotham scratched his bald spot for a moment.

"Yes, sir. Then we went into Bill and Nayda's—"

"Can these people verify that he was there?" he asked.

"Of course they can!" Alex replied firmly. "Kris is their friend. He's been going there for ten years."

"What time did you leave?" the principal demanded.

"Gosh, I don't know. I don't even know how long we were there. Let's see, there were three people in the diner when we got there. The guy in the overalls looked like he had already eaten dinner and was having coffee. But the two guys at the counter were just looking at menus. When we left, the diner was pretty empty."

She paused, then looked up at Mr. Higgenbotham and asked suddenly, "How long would it take for someone to order, eat dinner, and have dessert?"

"I—uh, I don't know," he replied, a little startled by the question.

"Well, that's how long we were there," Alex stated. "*Then*, we went home, and Kris walked me to the door and we talked for a while."

Alex paused for the briefest second as the image of Kris kissing her good night passed through her mind. She wondered if she should tell the principal of her school about a kiss— the kiss she could not stop thinking about. Then she blurted out, "Then he said good night and promised me he'd call. Which he never actually did. But—"

"I think I've heard enough, young lady!" Mr. Higgenbotham said severely. Alex felt her face flush crimson, and she stared down at her hands clasped tightly in her lap. She had squeezed them so hard that her nails had left little dents on her knuckles.

The principal pressed the button on his intercom and ordered, "Miss Wray, send Kris Van Dam in, please."

In a moment Alex heard the door to the office

open with a creak. There was Kris, standing right beside her.

"Sit down, Kris," Mr. Higgenbotham said, motioning to another chair. "This young lady has been giving me an intriguing account of your whereabouts Friday night."

Alex glanced up just as Kris was sitting down. He looked at her and nodded stiffly, then folded his hands. She looked back down at the floor.

"I must say," the principal continued, removing his glasses and rubbing his eyes wearily, "I'm a little confused about the exact sequence of events. She claims you went to, uh, Bill and—"

"Nayda's," Kris finished for him. "That's right, sir."

"And that you were supposed to call her that night, but didn't."

"No!" Alex said. "Not that night. The next day."

"But what does that have to do with Friday night?" Mr. Higgenbotham asked sharply.

Alex started to say, "Everything!" but stopped herself. She couldn't think of an answer, and Mr. Higgenbotham turned his attention to Kris.

"When you arrived home, were your parents there?"

"Yes, sir," Kris nodded. "I mean, my mother was, yes."

"I see. Well, if we can verify that you were indeed at the diner during the time in question, that would effectively clear you of any involvement in the events of Friday evening." Mr. Higgenbotham pushed his chair back and stepped to his office door. "You two are free to return to your classes. Miss Wray will write you passes. Good day."

Alex got up and moved shakily toward the door. Tears were riding dangerously close to the surface, and she knew that if she didn't get out of there quickly she might embarrass herself further. She took the pass from Miss Wray and collected her books that she'd left on the couch.

"I couldn't call!" Kris whispered hoarsely from behind her. "You aren't listed in the phone book."

"Then you should have come by," Alex said curtly, without looking at him.

"I couldn't," Kris protested. "I was away with my parents!"

"Oh, sure!" Alex rolled her eyes in disbelief. "A likely story!" Then she turned and looked him square in the face. "What about the note?" she hissed. Without waiting for an answer, Alex lifted her chin defiantly and pushed through the glass doors into the hall.

Kris was right behind her. "*What* note?"

"Ha!" Alex said over her shoulder. She stomped down the empty hall toward their locker, with Kris following at her heels.

"Alex?" he said, moving around in front of her and jogging backward. "What note?"

She stopped at the locker, put one hand on her hip, and said, "The little perfumed note that you had in your pocket!" With a sinking feeling, Alex realized she had just admitted to snooping through his personal belongings.

"Um, I couldn't help reading it," she said, looking down. "It just fell out of your vest by the locker, and—"

Kris was looking at her with a strange, blank expression.

"It doesn't matter, anyway," she said. "But it proves you lied to me!"

"Wait a minute, wait a minute!" Kris interjected. "What in the world are you talking about?"

"That note!" Alex said insistently. "From Megan!"

"Megan!" he said explosively, his eyes open wide.

"Yes, Megan," Alex said. "M. 'Yesterday was special. Love, M.' Remember?"

There was a sudden, eerie silence. Kris stood openmouthed, staring at her until it seemed his eyes would pop out of their sockets. She challenged his stare unblinkingly. Alex knew she had him then.

Then he began to laugh quietly. Little, hiccupping sounds soon grew into huge gasps of laughter. Tears began to stream out of his eyes, and Alex thought he must have lost his mind.

"What's so funny?" she demanded, dropping her arms to her sides.

"Everything!" he answered. "You, the note—everything." Finally Kris got his laughter under control. "Alex," he explained, "that note was from my mother."

"*What?*" Alex stepped back and fell against the locker. She blinked at him uncomprehendingly.

"Yes." Kris grinned, folding his arms. "And if you weren't so doggone stubborn, I could have explained that yesterday."

"Then why didn't you come by my house over the weekend, or leave a note, or something?"

"Because," he said gently, "I told you, I was with my parents. We left early Saturday morning for the mountains. It was on the spur of the moment."

"Oh!" Alex said meekly.

"My parents finally decided it was time for us all to talk. We spent the weekend together and made a lot of important decisions."

Alex swallowed hard. Then she asked hesitantly, "What did you decide?"

"Well." He took a deep breath and began carefully, "We decided that making me choose between parents wasn't very fair."

"Uh-huh," Alex agreed, urging him to continue.

"And moving to another state in my last two years of high school would be really hard for me."

Alex nodded, not daring to breathe.

"So"—Kris paused dramatically, his eyes sparkling—"it looks like I'll be staying here in Denver at Centennial High."

"Oh, Kris!" Alex dropped her books and threw her arms around his neck. She hugged him with all her might. Then, embarrassed, she stepped back. "I—I don't know what to say."

"Try not saying anything."

"What do you mean?" she asked innocently.

"Maybe"—Kris grinned—"you should just listen, for a change." He put his finger to her lips and continued, "If you hadn't gotten so mad, we wouldn't have had this misunderstanding in the first place."

She started to protest, but Kris silenced her with a look.

"If you and I are going to be together, we have to trust each other." He looked into her unblinking eyes and asked, "Understand?"

Alex nodded slowly.

"And if we have any problems, we talk to each other first, right?"

Alex crossed her heart with her right hand and held it up as if taking an oath.

"Good!" He smiled at her and then slowly took his hand away from her lips. "Now, do you have any questions?"

Alex nodded vigorously.

He gave her a crooked grin and asked, "What?"

"When you said the part about us being 'together,' " Alex asked, "did you mean *together*, or just—together?"

Kris raised an eyebrow, looking a little confused.

"What I mean is," Alex tried to explain clearly, "one kind of together is just sharing a locker and getting along as friends. And the other is, well, you know." She shrugged sheepishly. "Together."

Kris stared down at her, shaking his head in amazement. Finally he said, "I meant, together."

"*Together* together, or just—"

Alex never finished her sentence. As his lips met hers she wrapped her arms around his neck and in that wonderful moment, all her questions were answered.